"Out

Mary Louise demanded.

The secret suddenly seemed too large and too exciting for Spring to keep to herself. "I'm going to marry Reed," she responded softly.

The stunned silence that followed was finally broken by one awed question: "Has he asked you?"

Suddenly she felt foolish for having revealed her secret longing. "No," she admitted. Not only hadn't he asked, he didn't even know. She'd carefully hidden her feelings from him, along with the clamoring he'd caused in her heart since her sixteenth birthday.

Mary Louise snorted derisively. "Dare to dream," she snapped, and the other girls hooted.

"Ladies," the firm voice drifted down the hall, "would you kindly shut up? It's three o'clock in the morning."

"Who'd want him?" Mary Louise whispered.

Me, Spring thought firmly, and she didn't join in the giggles....

Dear Reader,

Welcome to Silhouette. Experience the magic of the wonderful world where two people fall in love. Meet heroines who will make you cheer for their happiness, and heroes (be they the boy next door or a handsome, mysterious stranger) who will win your heart. Silhouette Romances reflect the magic of love—sweeping you away with books that will make you laugh and cry, heartwarming, poignant stories that will move you time and time again.

In the next few months, we're publishing romances by many of your all-time favorites, such as Diana Palmer, Brittany Young, Emilie Richards and Arlene James. Your response to these authors and other authors of Silhouette Romances has served as a touchstone for us, and we're pleased to bring you more books with Silhouette's distinctive medley of charm, wit and—above all—*romance*.

I hope you enjoy this book and the many stories to come. Experience the magic!

Sincerely,

Tara Hughes
Senior Editor
Silhouette Books

CARA
COLTER
Dare
to Dream

Silhouette *Romance*

Published by Silhouette Books New York

America's Publisher of Contemporary Romance

To the Captain
Maurice J. Caron
the Okanagan's biggest fan, best fisherman,
and greatest father.

SILHOUETTE BOOKS
300 E. 42nd St., New York, N.Y. 10017

Copyright © 1987 by Cara Colter

ISBN: 0-373-08491-9

First Silhouette Books printing March 1987

America's Publisher of Contemporary Romance

Printed in the U.S.A.

CARA COLTER's

passion for writing led her to take a two-year journalism arts program. Though she graduated with flying colors, she admits that the program "took something I loved and turned it into a job." She's now been freelancing successfully for six years—by successfully, she means she's "never had to resort to the soup line!" But it wasn't until she discovered writing romances that the passion she felt for writing was returned to her. "I'm living where I want to live"—Canada's sunny Okanagan Valley—"and doing what I want to do."

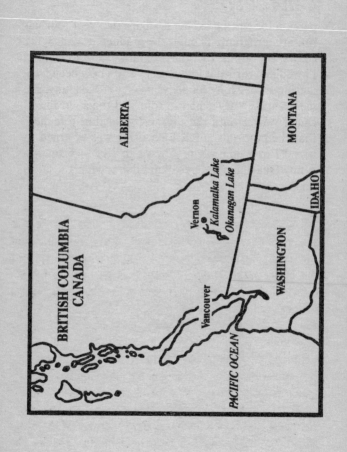

Chapter One

A single, tattered paper rattled against the branches of the small shrub that ensnared it. It was a frail sound in the nearly deserted streets of early morning Vancouver, but the young woman walking alone, her shoulders hunched against a raw wind, reacted as if a gun had gone off next to her ear. Like a startled rabbit, she bounded a few steps sideways, then turned and glared accusingly at the paper.

Spring O'Hara sighed, annoyed and embarrassed by her instinctive fearful reaction, and then smiled ruefully and continued on her way. Still, she couldn't help but send the occasional furtive glance over her shoulder, scanning the shadowed reality for the hulks of the muggers who stalked her in her imagination. Finally she caught sight of her own apartment building, broke into a trot, turned up the concrete path and inserted her key in the door. Once inside, she leaned on the door and closed her eyes as it clicked, comfortingly locking behind her.

"I should have taken a cab," she murmured softly, just as she did every morning. Her face darkened into an unconscious scowl. A cab, indeed! No matter how she dreaded these early morning walks or how many times her roommate tried to persuade her of the dangers of a solitary stroll in the wee hours, she simply couldn't afford to take a cab.

Spring pushed herself away from the door, unaware that her scowl deepened. The grim fact was that, despite a college education, she made minimum wage as a waitress in an all-night café, and cab fare would take an atrocious chunk out of her hard-earned wages.

She gave an indignant little sputter as she remembered just how hard-earned those wages were. Spring hated Cap's Café, with its tacky pink and purple plastic booths, harsh lights and all-pervasive smell of grease. And the late night clientele! Drunk, surly or demanding, and usually all three, not to mention notoriously bad tippers.

As if that wasn't bad enough, this morning, an hour before her shift drew to a merciful close, an obnoxious man with flushed cheeks and beady eyes had reached out and pinched her bottom. Hard! She had shrieked and whirled, dumping her whole tray of hot coffee on his lap, which she felt he richly deserved even if she hadn't done it on purpose. But the worst of it was that old Cap had yelled a string of colourful names at her, unheeding of justice—or of their amused audience.

Spring had been born and raised in Canada, but her father's Irish temper had boiled in her at the totally undeserved humiliation of the situation—and then, with superhuman effort she'd bitten it back. Jobs in the field she had trained in—bookkeeping—were impossible to come by lately, and even a job like this one was hard enough to find.

Setting her lips in a determined line, Spring forced the incident from her mind, channelling her thoughts instead to the awaited comfort of a hot shower, the warm welcome of her cozy bedroom and her soft bed.

She was still daydreaming about sweet-smelling sheets when she entered her apartment. Her pert nose wrinkled with disgust as it made the transition from the pleasant scents of her imagination to the reality of air heavy with the odours of smoke and stale liquor.

Carolyn had hosted another party, Spring surmised, walking down the hall and peeping warily into the living room. She groaned softly at the scattered debris—empty bottles, leftover bowls of food, overflowing ashtrays, records out of their jackets and potato chips carelessly ground into the carpet. With firm resolve she turned her back on the mess, marched to the bathroom and shut the door with a snap.

She eyed her reflection in the mirror wearily. She absently ran her fingers through a slightly tangled, sweeping mane of hair the colour of ripened wheat, and gave her head an unconscious scolding shake at the dark circles under her eyes and the well-defined hollows under her cheekbones that warned her she was far too thin.

"Beautiful," one of the customers had told her last night with drunken gallantry. "The most beautiful girl I've ever seen—and that ain't just booze talking, miss."

Spring regarded herself critically, trying to see what her admirer had seen. A very ordinary girl gazed back—a girl with a fragile bone structure, unhealthily pale skin, a slightly turned-up nose and a pointed chin. Nothing spectacular, she decided, though she admitted her eyes were unusual. She turned from the mirror muttering wryly, "Booze talking."

She was genuinely oblivious to the fact her eyes were astonishing, particularly in contrast to the gold of her hair and the milky white of her skin. They were enormous, round and black. Not the hard glittering black of obsidian, but rather the soft black of a summer-night sky, the velvety black found at the heart of a delicate wildflower.

Spring stripped her much-hated and now coffee-stained uniform off her willowy frame, adjusted the shower and stepped eagerly under the hot, massaging needles of water. She sighed happily as the greasy smell that seemed to permeate her very skin faded and then was gone. For the first time that morning she relaxed completely, letting the pummelling jets of water work soothing magic on the gentle curves of her aching and weary body.

Finally, in danger of falling asleep on her feet, she shut off the water, took her fluffy housecoat from its hook behind the door and wrapped it around herself. Yawning contentedly, she padded to her bedroom, having once again cleared her mind of everything but the welcome of her soft pillow and warm bed.

"Oh!" she gasped from her bedroom door, staring at her bed with wide-eyed dismay. A sleep-tousled blond head was visible above her comforter. Her dismay gave way to annoyance, and she strode over and glared down at the handsome male face. She recognized Carolyn's boyfriend, Rob, and gave him an impatient shake.

Rob groaned mightily and rolled over, the comforter slipping to reveal a broad and very naked chest. Spring leapt back from the bed, regarding her intruder warily. What if he wasn't wearing anything at all? Her cheeks brightened to crimson at the thought, and she reluctantly retreated from her bedroom.

Her bedroom! she thought grouchily as she sat on the couch in the living room, nibbling absently on the remains of some chips and dip. Suddenly she felt her lip begin to tremble with weariness and frustration.

I can't stand it, she thought despairingly. I can't stand this city. It's too big and noisy, bustling and frightening. And I can't stand my job. And now my last sanctuary—my own bed—has been invaded.

Spring O'Hara, she warned herself, you stop it right now! Or in a minute you'll be thinking of home. And then she realized she already was thinking of home, and the tears began to sting behind the thick, tangled curtain of her black lashes.

You don't have a home, she reminded herself fiercely. There's been no home for three years. But instead of dispelling the tears, her grim reminder only brought them closer to the surface.

Okay, Spring, she addressed herself sternly, enough self-pity. If reminding yourself that you haven't got a home won't stop this pathetic flow of self-pity, just think of *him*.

Slowly the tears stopped threatening, and the lump in her throat faded, replaced by a disciplined coldness. The hate she felt, and the bitter anger, were far preferable to helpless tears. With the familiar image of the man who had betrayed her foremost in her mind, Spring plumped a sofa cushion furiously, laid down her head and fell into an exhausted and dreamless sleep.

Spring awoke to the sound of someone pounding insistently on the apartment door. She waited drowsily and hopefully for Carolyn to answer it or for whoever it was to give up and go away. Realizing both her hopes were in vain, Spring muttered a mild oath, pulled her housecoat tight around her and went to the door.

The landlord, she guessed, her hand on the knob. She braced herself to listen to his loud, if justified, complaints about the party last night and flung open the door.

But no amount of preparation could have braced her for the man who stood before her. His height and his broad shoulders blocked out the dim light in the hall behind him, and Spring unconsciously sucked in her breath, unable to speak, and even less able to unfasten her eyes from his face.

Hungrily her eyes insisted on tracing the familiar plains of his features. He was the same, she thought hazily. His eyes were still as green as jade, his thick mahogany hair still looking like it had just been shoved impatiently off his forehead. The jutting chin, the well-defined nose, the prominent cheekbones, the deep, deep tan of a man who had spent all his life outdoors—all were the same, she thought, with a small frown, and yet different, too. His eyes seemed cooler, somehow, than she had remembered them—cooler, and sterner, and infinitely more weary. There were tiny somber creases around his mouth that had never been there before, and with a small shiver of shock, she realized the hair at his temples held threads of silver.

Only three years, she thought, feeling a wild and absurdly tender impulse to lift her hand to his face, as if the light touch of her fingertips could erase the changes she found there.

She quelled the impulse, and her eyes trailed helplessly down the lean and muscled length of his body. How well she remembered the dark hair, silky and sensual, that sprang from the V of his shirt collar, the immense broadness of his chest and shoulders, the suggestion of raw strength in the rippling line of his arms, even when they were relaxed at his sides, as they were now.

There was no sign of age thickening the flat contours of his waistline and no mistaking the outline of hard muscle beneath the taut fabric of clean, faded blue jeans. His body seemed unchanged from that day she had first seen him, all those years ago, and somehow that didn't surprise her. She let her gaze slip up to encounter the devastating deep green of his eyes.

He'd made no attempt to break the silence between them, and now she became aware that he was studying her with at least the same intensity she'd given him. His gaze came to rest on the dark, smudgy shadows beneath her eyes, and for a breathless moment she was certain he was going to reach out tenderly and trace those lines, as if he wished to erase the evidence of life's haggardness from her face, just as she had wished she could erase it from him. But instead, a curtain of coolness fell smoothly over his eyes, and the creases around his mouth deepened disapprovingly.

"Reed," she whispered, and the spell she had been under shattered painfully at the mention of his name. Only this morning she had conjured up the stunning sense of betrayal and hatred she felt for him and those feelings returned and swept over her now. For a moment she debated whether to slam the door in his face, but the stern light deepened in his eyes, giving Spring the uneasy sensation that he had read her mind.

"What do you want?" she demanded, hoping she sounded cool and composed, *and* older than her twenty-one years.

His face tautened, almost imperceptibly. "I wasn't quite sure," he said in a flat, hard voice, "until I saw your face. You look wretched. Have you been ill?"

Spring mastered the childish urge to stamp her foot. The audacity of the man! To march into her life unannounced after a three-year absence, inspect her for three seconds and pronounce with insufferable arrogance that she looked wretched! The fact that she had reached much the same conclusion herself earlier this morning conveniently slipped her mind.

"No, I haven't been ill," she snapped, "but thanks for the compliment. I'm sure it will make my day."

He regarded her lazily, unmoved by her outburst. "I don't have much patience with small talk or false flattery, Spring. You should know that." He glanced meaningfully over her shoulder. "May I come in?"

"Are you asking?" she shot back, her tone dripping with exaggerated incredulity.

For the first time a small smile touched his firm lips, but it didn't reach his eyes, and it wasn't particularly pleasant.

It was clear he wasn't asking, and Spring rigidly held open the door to let him pass, grinding her teeth seethingly when he gave her a curt, slightly mocking nod as he brushed by her.

He sniffed the air quizzically, like a wolf lifting its muzzle to the wind, and the lines of disapproval around his mouth deepened. He stopped again at the archway into the living room, his eyes flicking disdainfully from the empty bottles to the full ashtrays.

For a moment he said nothing, his silence screaming across Spring's taut nerves. Then she was treated to the full impact of his blazing eyes.

"What the hell kind of life are you leading, Spring?" he demanded, his voice a soft, angry hiss.

To her horror the sharp "It's none of your damn business" that he deserved to hear was trapped in her throat somewhere, and it was a strangled sob that emerged from her lips. She pushed by him and sank down onto the couch, trying valiantly to staunch the unexpected flow of tears. But her tears had been kept on a tight leash too long; and now freed, they stubbornly resisted her efforts to bring them under control.

With the unconscious carriage and grace of an athlete, Reed lowered his body into the chair opposite her and regarded her, his green eyes narrowly impassive and without sympathy.

Suddenly, through the misty curtain of her tears, Spring saw Rob coming down the hallway, clad only in his blue jeans and rubbing his eyes blearily. He stopped just short of the archway, becoming aware of her. He cocked a puzzled brow at her, and then grinned with all his considerable charm.

"Spring, angel! This is a crashing blow to my ego. I mean, I've had many reactions to women finding me in their beds, but nobody has ever cried before!" His grin widened with mock wolfishness.

Spring stared at him, aghast, and then looked quickly at Reed. The fury that had darkened the rugged lines of his face was nothing less than frightening, and she looked back at Rob, trying to impart to him silent warning.

But Rob had only noticed her quick, darting glance until he peered around the corner. "Oh-oh," he said cheerfully to Reed. "Who are you?"

"I might ask you the same question," Reed commented, a fine tension running just below the surface of the control in his deep voice.

Rob glanced at Spring. She was unaware that the tears trickling down her cheeks made her look ridiculously waiflike and woebegone and so the sudden emotion in Rob's face baffled her. Rob looked uncharacteristically angry and protective. As fiercely protective as a mountain lion with a cub. Missing her renewed look of warning completely, he glared accusingly into Reed's icy features.

"I'm Spring's fiancé," he announced cockily.

Spring's jaw dropped, and she stared at Rob with disbelief, then looked frantically at Reed and laughed shakily through her tears. "Oh, Reed, that's just not true. I barely know him."

Reed cocked a thunderous brow at her. "My," he said sardonically, "that paints a much prettier picture."

Spring felt the blood drain from her face and saw Rob's expression darken.

"Just who are you?" Rob demanded, then looked as if he immediately regretted his tone, as if he had become aware of the other man's intimidatingly well-muscled frame for the first time. Spring was aware of something vaguely dangerous glittering in the icy depths of Reed's eyes.

"I'm Spring's guardian."

Rob stared at him stupidly. "Oh-oh," he finally offered weakly. "Look, it wasn't true. About me being in Spring's bed. I mean I was, but it wasn't like..." He stopped, floundering under the effect of a rather large hangover and managing to make himself, and Spring, look guiltier than hell. "I mean—"

Spring saw the terrible expression in Reed's face and could see the tension beginning to coil warningly along the hard length of him. "Rob, shut up! Please, you're not helping at all. Just go!" And fast, if you know what's good for you, she added to herself, glancing again at the hard warning chiselled into Reed's features.

"Wonderful idea," Rob said, sending her an apologetic glance that did nothing to hide his relief at being excused. He turned hastily from them, and a few minutes later the apartment door shut behind him. Spring's tears were under control now, and she faced Reed stoically, her nose turned up with dignity that denied her earlier tears.

Suddenly he spoke, and though his voice was low and controlled, to Spring it seemed like an explosion had gone off in the small room.

"Who is he, Spring?"

"He's my room—"

Reed's harsh ejaculation cut her off rudely, and Spring felt her temper beginning to rise. How dare he jump to the conclusion Rob was her roommate! How dare he want to think the worst of her so badly that she wasn't even allowed to finish her sentences! Well, if that's what he wanted to believe, let him!

Her chin came up with proud defiance. "Reed, it's none of your business who he is, or what he means to me. And how dare you tell him that you're my guardian? You're not! I'm twenty-one. I'm legally of age, and your obligation to me is long over—thank God for small mercies!"

Reed came swiftly out of his chair, and Spring shrank back from the violence that seemed to tingle like static in the air around him. He turned his broad back to her abruptly, thrusting his clenched fists deep into his jean pockets. For an endless moment he stared silently out the window at the black ridges of the mountains that ringed Vancouver and soared above the jagged apartment rooftops.

When he turned back to her the violence had ebbed out of him. "Get your things, Spring," he said wearily. "I'm taking you home."

For a moment she was too stunned by his cool pronouncement to respond—but only for a moment.

"Taking me home?" she rasped, and then laughed, the sound bitter and brittle in her own ears. "I don't have a home, Reed. You whipped that out from underneath me three years ago. I told you then that I'd never go back, not if you got down on one knee and begged me. And I won't!" The tears and her fear of him had evaporated, replaced with an angry fire that flashed deep in the inky depths of her eyes.

He was at her in a single stride, and she found her shoulders caught painfully in the grip of strong fingers. His eyes flicked over her face, lashing her with the force of a whip. But despite that, Spring refused to flinch or struggle, meeting his angry, sparking eyes evenly.

"But I'm not begging you," he informed her softly, through clenched teeth, "I'm telling you."

"And I'm telling you—I'm an adult. And I have no home." She corrected herself quickly. "I mean that my home is here."

He let her go suddenly, and she stubbornly refused to acknowledge that the touch of his hands, even in anger, had aroused a searing heat inside of her. Rage, she convinced herself, that's what this all-consuming fire is....

"Let's cut the melodrama," he ordered impatiently, his voice once again controlled, though Spring could detect a threatening thread running through it. "I did not toss you out on your ear, and I have no idea why you cling to that idea with such stubborn fondness. You were sent to school, which I naively believed was the best way to prepare you for the adult world." His eyes narrowed on the debris scattered around the living room. "Though now I have my severe doubts about the wisdom of that decision.

"But to come back to the point, Spring, I didn't turn my back on you. If anything it was the other way around. I sent you the airfare to come home at least ten times in the past three years. Each time it was returned with a crisp little note that you had other plans. I wrote, and my letters weren't answered. I phoned to see how you were doing, and you wouldn't talk to me. I've waited patiently for you to outgrow this childish feud you're engaged in all by yourself. But my patience—which was never one of my strong points to begin with—has just reached an end. You're coming home."

Spring stared at him. How could he do this? How could he twist things so that she came out looking like the villain? And almost feeling like the villain? But suddenly she recalled that last violent scene with him. Recalled tearfully begging him, recalled presenting him with a hundred alternatives to sending her away. She flushed, now, remembering what one of those alternatives had been, recalling how cruelly he had looked at her, how coldly he had dismissed her arguments.

"I hate you, Reed," she spat at him. "Can't you understand that? I'm not going with you."

Something flickered in his eyes, then he shrugged, dismissing the depth of her emotion with infuriating ease. "How you feel about me is inconsequential. I'm responsible for you until the day I feel you can be responsible for yourself." His eyes rested once again on the dark crescents under her eyes as if they provided all the necessary evidence of her inability to take care of herself. She started to speak, but he cut her off.

"Your legal age means nothing to me, Spring, and I have no interest in hearing again that you're an amazingly mature lady of twenty-one."

"You can't make me come with you," she sputtered, annoyed at having been read so easily.

"You...are...coming...home. You can come willingly, or unwillingly, but you are coming." The words were spoken with absolute and utterly maddening confidence. Reed glanced at his watch. "I'll give you half an hour to pack your things."

"And if I don't?" Spring demanded hotly. "Then what, Reed? Are you going to tie me up, gag me, throw me in the trunk of your car and drive away?"

"Naturally," he replied dryly, and for the first time she saw a glimmer of genuine amusement in his eyes, as if he were dealing with a difficult child and these contests of will were slightly amusing for their complete lack of competition.

"You egotistical, arrogant, boorish, insulting—"

"Twenty-nine minutes." He cut her off, without consulting his watch.

She glared at him, then with an exclamation of pure disgust bounced up off the sofa and marched by him with her head held high. She went into her bedroom and slammed the door, wishing fervently that it had a lock on it, glanced at it again, and decided that a mere lock wouldn't provide much of a barrier against Reed if he decided he wanted to come in.

She sank onto her bed, her mind reeling from one crazy unviable escape plan to another. A knock interrupted her, and she looked around wildly for a place to hide. Her half hour couldn't be up. What did he want now?

"Spring, can I come in?" It was Carolyn, and Spring sighed with relief. Carolyn came in, her dark hair sleep tousled but her blue eyes wide open and full of curiosity.

"What's going on around here this morning? Rob didn't even say goodbye. And who is the fire-eating dragon in the living room? I just poked my head in and said good-morning, and he kind of growled at me. Handsome devil, I must say."

"That's Reed," Spring responded dully.

Her friend looked at her with surprise. "Reed? Reed Caldwell? But Spring, whenever you've mentioned him I was left with the impression he was old, and a bit of an ogre." She giggled. "Okay, I'll buy the ogre part. But old? Honest to God, Spring, he's devastating."

"He is old," Spring snapped. "He's thirty-one. And devastating is exactly the right word for him. He wanders around and devastates people's lives—especially mine!" she finished with a wail.

"Tell me what's going on," Carolyn persuaded her gently.

Slowly Spring told her the whole story. About Reed arriving unexpectedly and finding the apartment in a shambles and her in a shambles, and then about Rob's unexpected appearance and his highly suggestive remarks. "And now," she concluded despondently, "Reed says I have to go home. Oh, Carolyn, what am I going to do?"

Carolyn looked at her thoughtfully, then smiled affectionately. "You're going to go home."

"What!" Spring exclaimed with horrified dismay. "I can't! You don't understand at all!" She had expected Carolyn, who had been her roommate through a number of years and different situations, to understand.

"Listen to me, Spring," Carolyn insisted with patient firmness. "Go home. The game's up. You don't belong here. You don't belong in a place like Cap's Café, and you don't belong with people like Rob and me, and Sharon and Fran. We're all wild—parties, and pubs and good times. I suspect you're more suited to curling up beside a fire with a book and acres of snowy silence or blossoming apple trees all around you.

"You're too gentle for life here, too sensitive, and in the oddest way more grown-up than us. Don't look so surprised. It's true. In maturity you outstrip us all by a million miles. I always knew that, even when you first arrived at St. Lucias to finish off your last few months of high school. There was something about you that was sad, wise and infinitely adult. It was as if you knew something about love and life that the rest of us hadn't discovered yet. Go home, Spring."

"I don't have a home, Carolyn," Spring stated wearily.

Carolyn nodded slowly. "Yes, I've heard you say that before. But I've also seen the look in your eyes when someone comes home from a holiday in the Okanagan Valley, and when they start to talk about the sun, the hills, the lakes . . . and the orchards." She smiled kindly. "It's there right now, a kind of wistful, aching sadness that makes my heart break for you." She paused, looking at Spring intently. "It's blossom time, isn't it?"

Blossom time. Dully, Spring admitted some mental calendar inside her had known. Yet consciously she had avoided its knowing. Avoided it because of the yearning the visions of the orchards in springtime could cause within her. She nodded faintly at Carolyn, feeling absurdly close to tears again, feeling as if the faint, subtle aroma of apple blossoms had crept into the room. Still, she shook her head. "I can't—"

Carolyn sighed impatiently. "Go! Don't you think he knew, the minute he looked at your face, how unhappy you've been? Rob probably just gave him an excuse to do what he really wanted to do anyway. I bet you belong there, and I'll bet he knows it. I bet you know it too, deep in your heart. Maybe that's why you look so sad sometimes—because you're fighting something you shouldn't fight."

Spring looked at her roommate sharply. Could Carolyn know? But of course she couldn't. How could she know about a young girl falling sweetly, helplessly and hopelessly in love with a man who had taken that love and crushed it?

How could Spring ever go back? How, when the only happiness she'd ever known was given to her by the hand of the same man who'd come to give bitterness and betrayal?

Spring frowned. Had Carolyn been right? Had Reed really seen how unhappy she was? But that would imply compassion, and she knew, from experience, that he had none. No, she decided, it was responsibility. Duty. Even an old-fashioned word like *honour* applied well to Reed. He did everything he did well, from growing apples to swimming, to playing the guitar. It would be a personal affront to his pride if the girl he had helped to raise didn't meet his high standards.

And yet Carolyn had made a point. Spring knew she didn't belong here. Maybe it was time to go back and find out where she did belong. Maybe it was time to go back and see if the sweet joy of her childhood had been entirely illusion—Lord knows she had felt no joy here in this rainy city. Was she really willing to live without that?

Maybe it was time to face those painful and shadowy ghosts. Spring knew with sudden clarity that happiness would continue to elude her until she did that, until she put the childish dreams and nightmares to rest once and for all.

She was surprised how even considering the possibility of going home did something to her: filled her with a strange and reluctant elation, an eagerness that she didn't want to feel, and yet couldn't suppress. And then she knew. She would go home. With that decision, a sudden lightness danced through her, and though she wasn't prepared to admit it, it might have been some small remembrance of what it was to be joyful.

A streak of stubborn pride refused her to allow Reed the satisfaction of knowing how she really felt, so when she faced him half an hour later, her eyes were deliberately chilly and she held her head at a haughty angle.

"I'm ready," she said coolly.

"Good." He didn't even have the decency to look slightly surprised by her compliance.

"You can make me go with you, Reed. I refuse to be dragged screaming to the car. But you can't make me stay. The first time you turn your back, I could leave."

It was a weak attempt to defy his power, and even knowing that, she could have slapped him for the amusement that danced in his eyes. The stern anger of earlier was far preferable.

"Yes, you could," he answered quietly, his tone infuriatingly patronizing.

"Well, I could!" she said sharply, just as if he hadn't agreed with her, which of course he really hadn't.

His face remained solemn, though the knowing light in his eyes mocked her. He reached for her case, and she jerked it away from him.

"I can take it myself."

"You could," he said, and she knew he was not just referring to the suitcase, "but you won't." He reached around her easily, wrested the case from her firm grip, and strode out the door, leaving her to trail after him feeling like a silly puppy.

He still drove "Maude," a silver-grey Mercedes sports coupe, but Spring refused to comment, even if it was like seeing an old friend. Instead she slipped wordlessly by him when he held open the door for her and settled herself in the deep, comfortable leather seat. In fact, setting her lips in a firm line, she decided not to say another word to him all the way home, and Vernon was a good seven hours from Vancouver.

The arrangement didn't seem to disturb him. He manoeuvred through the Vancouver streets silently, concentrating on the traffic, and acting as if he wasn't even aware he had a sulky, seething passenger in the seat beside him.

They were only a few miles out of the city when Spring realized she was going to have to break her self-imposed vow of silence. The tension of the morning seemed to have settled somewhere in the region of her stomach, and suddenly, squeamishly, she remembered that awful unrefrigerated dip she had eaten so absently in the early hours.

"Reed," she said weakly, "you have to stop. I'm going to be sick."

He shot her an assessing look and pulled swiftly onto the shoulder, leaning across her and flinging open her door. Spring stumbled unseeingly from the car and went to her knees, suddenly aware of Reed behind her, his hand moving soothingly along the back of her neck while her stomach heaved. Later he helped her up, handed her a handkerchief and impersonally stowed her into the car. She felt confused. His hand on her neck had been so comforting, such a gentle gesture of compassion. And it had seemed to come from him so naturally....

"Let's hope it's not morning sickness," Reed muttered tersely, revving the powerful engine and pulling back into traffic.

The words left Spring confused. "Morning sickness?" she echoed, stunned, and then she blushed. "That's impossible," she spat out heatedly.

"Even the pill isn't one hundred percent," he informed her flatly. He seemed angry again, his face stony, denying that there had been any tenderness in his gesture of a few minutes ago.

What about virginity? she wanted to hurl at him, but she bit it back. Let Reed think what he wanted. Why not let him assume she was worldly and experienced? Maybe then he wouldn't treat her like such a kid. Besides, what if she told him the truth, and he didn't believe her? That would be far more humiliating than letting him just go on thinking what he wanted. I hate him, she thought angrily, feeling betrayed by him all over again.

"It is a terrible thought," she said sweetly, "another generation of O'Hara children looking at poor Reed Caldwell adoringly, following him around, getting in his way...." She watched his reaction covertly from the corner of her eye, but instead of feeling satisfied, she winced as she saw the lines around his mouth whiten.

"Don't...you...ever," he said slowly and harshly, his voice little more than a whisper, "say anything like that again."

Spring stared down at her hands. "I won't." It was terrible, she realized, to want to hurt someone so badly that you could take something that had been good and sweet and loving and try to turn it ugly. She meant it—she wouldn't do that again. For all that had occurred later, her childhood was a sacred ground that she didn't want to desecrate, and she found it vaguely reassuring that Reed also viewed those memories with sanctity.

She glanced at his stern, formidable profile and sighed. There had been a time when it was almost impossible to picture Reed without a boyish grin playing across his handsome, tanned face, a time when the glow of mischievous laughter was never far from his eyes.

But that was so long ago, she reminded herself sadly. Is there anything left, she asked herself, of the two people that we used to be?

The thought made her heavy with a weariness that twenty-one-year-olds usually don't know. She closed her eyes, wanting to escape into sleep, but her mind's eyes pictured a little girl in worn coveralls, dancing happily to the silent music of the breeze rustling through the apple trees.

The man had come, and they had both frozen, eyeing each other with wary surprise. Then he had walked slowly up to her, and crouched down in front of her, touching her fat, clumsily done braids as if assuring himself that she was real and not some woodland nymph. He'd smiled suddenly, revealing straight, wonderfully white teeth, and his eyes had reached out to her. She'd stared at him, amazed by the colour of those eyes. Suddenly she was not in the least afraid of him, for all her daddy's warnings about strangers and truant officers.

"And who are you?" he'd asked her, and she saw his eyes smiled even when his lips had stopped. She smiled back, trusting him.

"I'm Spring," she announced boldly. "I'm six." She held up five fingers to prove it to him.

"Spring," he echoed softly, and the warm smile deepened in his eyes.

And so it began, Spring thought, listening to the deep purr of Maude's engine. So it began....

Chapter Two

Something gently commanded her to wake up. Had it really been warm breath fanning across her cheek and then lips brushing hers with incredible tenderness? Half-asleep, Spring lingered dreamily for a moment in that thought. Then she realized that the hum of the car's engine had stopped. It must have been the car, she thought regretfully, that had awoken her. The other was just a dream.

She opened her eyes slowly and blinked at Reed. His face was close to hers, as if indeed he might have kissed her, and she allowed herself the sleepy luxury of studying him, studying the sweep of his ridiculously long eyelashes, the arch of his dark brows and the faint, shadowy traces of a beard appearing on his jaw and cheeks. Finally, she looked into his eyes and felt certain she saw a hint of tenderness mellowing them to a rich, warm green, both mysterious and inviting. But she blinked again, and the look in his eyes was gone. She must have dreamed it, willed it to be, because now that she was fully awake, she could see his features were inscrutable. Besides, she reminded herself irritably, Reed was not capable of the kind of tenderness she'd dreamed.

"Where are we?" she asked, tearing her eyes from his face and peering out the window. "Oh!"

"That's right, almost home. I thought you might want to stop here." His voice, not his words, aroused an ache in her that she didn't fully comprehend—a half-realized awareness of something infinitely appealing about masculine company and deep, velvety voices. She felt suddenly uncomfortable.

"I slept the whole way? I can barely believe it—" but even as she spoke, she was getting out of the car, dismissing that gnawing awareness and taking in the soft, intense blue of twilight with delighted wonder. She walked to the low stone wall. They were at the Kalamalka Lake Lookout, a highway viewpoint carved out of the hill high above the lake. From where she stood, she could look miles back down the lake that they had passed while she slept. The mountains and hills that rose up on either side of the lake and finally faded into the distance were hazy in the soft blue light, oddly mystical, as if they ringed and protected an enchanted land of fantasies and fairy tales.

Her gaze swung the other way, and she gasped, unable to contain her awed reaction. Reed was standing quietly beside her. The lights flickered on in the houses that lined the lakeshore and hills behind it. The lake mirrored them faithfully, turning the lights into dancing diamonds set in black velvet.

"I remember reading somewhere that this was one of the ten most beautiful views in the world," she breathed. "At the time, I thought the Vernon Chamber of Commerce was probably being overly ambitious. I'd forgotten. How could I forget my Lake of Many Colours?" The phrase was not a translation of Kalamalka, which had been named after the son of a respected Polynesian settler, but rather a pet name that the locals used in reference to the amazing array of colours produced by the deep lake, from a thousand subtle shades of green, turquoise and indigo to midnight blue.

"Careful, Spring," Reed remarked, his voice faintly teasing. "I'd almost think you were glad to be home. But of course, that's not possible, is it?"

"No, it's not," she retorted, but not with the conviction she would have liked. She had been on the verge of commenting on how lovely it was outside, the air as warm and comfortable as an embrace, but now she bit her tongue and turned instead for the car.

"Which way do you want to go?" Reed asked, starting the engine. "Do you want to take a tour of Main Street or take the shortcut down Kickwillie Loop Road?"

She didn't hesitate, though her choice meant that she would miss coming over the final rise in the road and seeing Vernon clustered comfortably along the valley floor between the hills and mountains that ringed it on all sides.

"Kickwillie!" she said, and was annoyed with herself when Reed laughed softly at her childlike enthusiasm. When she was small, she'd thought the trip down the steep twisting hill was like a ride on a roller coaster, and she would always rattle off her latest theory about the unusual name. Her favorite was that a man named Willie had been kicked by a mule here.

Reed's father had told her one day that long before the township of Vernon had been established, the Okanagan Indians had used the area as a winter gathering place.

They lived in *kekulis*—pits covered over with boughs and mud, that they went down into by means of a ladder. Kickwillie was just an anglicization of the Okanagan word for their dwelling places.

"Oh, Bo," Spring had said to Bob Caldwell, "that's nice but not nearly as much fun as thinking a man named Willie was kicked by his mule here." She giggled. "Reed says maybe it wasn't his mule at all—that maybe it was his wife."

"Reed said that, did he?" Bob Caldwell looked amused. And when she was a little older, Reed would admit that he had known all along....

"It doesn't seem as steep as it used to," Spring commented, almost to herself, as they wound down the hill.

"A lot of the things of childhood don't look nearly so big or so terrible through adult eyes, Spring."

"Really?" she said coolly, deliberately not responding to his double meaning. He meant, of course, that one day she wouldn't think it so terrible that he had sent her away, that when she was grown-up, she would understand. How hateful! Didn't he realize that she was grown-up? And that it could never seem less terrible?

She looked out the window, much of her pleasure gone as they drove by the public beach at the tip of Kalamalka Lake. Night was falling rapidly, and it was completely dark when Reed turned off the main road onto a gravel lane. And then they turned again, onto an even narrower gravel lane, and Spring felt her heart rise in her throat. They passed through two gateposts, and the headlights bounced off a sign nailed to one of them. It was faded and old, displaying big, absurdly curly letters painted with what had obviously been a juvenile hand. Orchard Hollow, it read.

"Why don't you take that ridiculous sign down?" Spring asked querulously, hoping her tone would disguise the emotion that was tugging at her heart. She well remembered the afternoons spent, her tongue between her teeth, working on that sign as a gift for Reed. She remembered the pride that had swollen inside her when he liked it and insisted on hanging it on the front gate.

"Because I still like it," Reed responded blandly.

They were in the orchard now, the lane lined on both sides with row upon endless row of blossoming apple trees. The moon was huge and bright. It had stripped the world of colour, leaving instead a fairyland of silvers and blacks.

"Please stop the car, Reed," she whispered. He glanced at her and without comment brought the car to a halt. She opened her door and stepped out, her senses reaching out eagerly to the magnificent sights all around her and the wonderful scent of the blossoms hanging heavy in the night air. She stood without moving for a long time, then turned to him.

"Go ahead, Reed," she said softly. "I'm going to walk."

"Do you want me to come?"

For a moment she thought she heard a note of exquisite gentleness in that deep, mellow voice. But no, she told herself, it was only a part of the magic that sang and danced through the warm spring air. She shook her head to his offer.

"Okay." He reached over and closed her door, started to drive away and then stopped. He got out and stood looking across the roof of the car at her. After a long time he said, "The bees are in, Spring. Don't go bumping into any hives." He looked at her a moment longer, then slipped into the car and drove away.

Funny, she thought, how that little warning drew her back, reminding her of a pool of knowledge that had lain dormant within her for three years, knowledge that came back to her now with comforting clarity and made her feel a part of this orchard, made her feel that she belonged.

The bees were brought in at the first sign of the king blossom opening. Apple blossoms grew in clusters of five, and the king blossom was the one in the centre. It always opened first, and it was the king blossom that you wanted the bees to pollinate. The pollinated blossoms became known as sets, and later, through sprays and by hand the sets would be thinned, leaving only a selected number to bear fruit.

Spring sighed, hugging herself. It seemed like she'd been born knowing that, the knowledge far more natural to her than the various skills she'd picked up for coping with life in a girl's school, then at college and finally in Vancouver.

She dropped her arms, delighting in the silence around her. No cars, no sirens, nothing at all but the faintest whisper of a breeze through the blossoms.

She moved off the road and into the orchard, unaware of the tears that shone in her soft black eyes. She reached up and touched a cluster of blossoms with caressing hands, then strolled on slowly, totally absorbed in the scents, sights and sounds that seemed to reach out and wrap themselves around her. She made her way up a slight knoll, looking down from the top over the acres of silver-washed apple trees.

In the hollow, far below her, she could see the house. It was a wonderful house—nearly eighty-five years old, nestled solidly on a square of grass, surrounded on three sides by the orchards. On the other side was a small pasture and some outbuildings and then orchard again.

The house was large and classic in design. A veranda, which ended at each corner with a rounded section like a small teahouse, dominated the design. But no less charming were the gables of the second-floor bedrooms or the dozens of large French-style windows with their tiny panes of glass.

Lights showing from all those windows sent cheery splashes of colour over the lawn and painted the blossoms of the apple trees bordering the yard golden. The lights seemed to be winking at her with a promise of warmth and welcome. With her hair flying behind her, and tears streaming down her cheeks, Spring ran through the canopied aisle of apple trees, down the hill. Toward home.

She arrived at the house out of breath, paused for a moment outside the back door and wiped hastily at her cheeks. She frowned uncertainly. Would Reed be busy telling Mrs. Kwolowski, the housekeeper, all about the wild life-style he'd found Spring living in Vancouver? She couldn't bear it if Mrs. K's worn, lovable face wore an expression of censure.

Quietly, almost timidly, Spring opened the squeaky back screen door, stepping directly into a cozy country kitchen. Reed was seated at the old, round oak table, a mug of steaming coffee in front of him. Mrs. K was busy at the stove, chattering away over her shoulder. She stopped at the sound of the door thumping closed and looked around with puzzlement. For a moment she said absolutely nothing, her mouth hanging open with surprise. And then the loveliest smile Spring had ever seen creased the leathery old face.

"Spring!" she cried, and flung open her arms, meeting Spring halfway cross the kitchen floor and hugging her to her bony frame with unbelievable strength. "Spring! I can't believe it. It's really you! Oh, but you're a sight for sore eyes . . . and imagine that scamp Reed not telling me he'd brought you home!"

Spring smiled and looked at Reed gratefully over Mrs. K's shoulder, feeling that she owed him at least that for keeping Vancouver between the two of them. He smiled back, and his face looked more relaxed than it had all day, making him look younger, more approachable—and dangerously handsome.

Imagine anybody calling him a scamp, she thought with a tiny shiver, turning her attention abruptly away from the compelling sight of him.

"Now, let's have a look at you," Mrs. K commanded, releasing her and studying her with sharp blue eyes. "Oh, child, you're too thin! And you look so tired!" She turned and looked at Reed accusingly. "I told you it was nonsense to allow this child to go to work in Vancouver. Dreadful place. No place for our girl at all. And you," she said, turning sternly to Spring, "should have come straight home the minute you graduated from school. Reed said that you were old enough to make up your own mind, but I didn't buy that! Not for one second did I buy that! A young girl like you fending for herself in that big city. It made me shudder—" Mrs. K demonstrated her shudder "—just to think about it. 'Reed,' I said, 'do you think they taught that girl to take care of herself in that fancy college? Do you think they taught her how to cook, how to find a job or how to protect herself from scoundrels?' But Reed said it was something we had to let you do—something young people have to get out of their systems. He said it was a good thing for you to test your independence before you settled down, and he said we had to trust you. 'Spring's a sensible girl,' he said. Ha! Sensible, my foot. Fanciful, imaginative and not a practical bone in your body. And I can tell from the look of you, you weren't living sensibly, not one little bit.

"Well, you're home now," Mrs. K said with heartfelt relief, "and I'll have you fattened up and looking healthy in no time...."

But Spring wasn't really listening. Puzzlement in her eyes, she was looking at Reed. Was what Mrs. K was saying true? Had he really defended her and believed in her? She felt suddenly stricken that she had disappointed him, let him down. Maybe she should set the record straight right now and let Reed know things were not exactly as they appeared in Vancouver. But weren't they? Reed wouldn't exactly be delighted if he found out she'd been working in an all-night café—especially since she'd written home that she was working in an office. He'd be enraged if he knew she'd lied and more enraged if he ever found out about those scary walks home in the mornings.

Besides, why should she take Mrs. K's word for it that he'd been all for trusting her? He'd yet to actually show her that he felt any faith in her at all. Maybe later, if they ever recaptured the closeness they had once shared, she would tell him the truth.

What am I thinking? she wondered wildly. I hate this man, and I'm thinking about closeness. Am I that much a fool that I would encourage closeness with Reed again? That I would leave myself vulnerable to him again? No, she decided with desperation, I couldn't survive it again. Better that she encourage the dislike she'd seen in his eyes this morning. Better that he believe the worst of her and treat her with contempt and disdain. That would be far easier to handle than his affection, far easier!

"Really, Mrs. K, I don't think that you should start making plans to fatten me up. I'm not sure how long I'll be here. Vancouver's very exciting, you know, and I just don't know how long I'll be able to last in this lazy little backwater." Spring thought that sounded suitably sophisticated, though she was a little surprised by how much the lie hurt to tell. Still, she saw Reed looking at her with dark annoyance etched into his face, and she pushed on, though she refused to meet his gaze for fear he would see the lie in her eyes.

"And of course," she continued with a sigh, "I'll miss Rob dreadfully." That should cinch it, she thought, but her satisfaction was oddly grim.

Mrs. K was looking at her skeptically. "Who's Rob?" she finally asked.

"Oh, he's just a friend," Spring claimed breezily, and then did her best to look dreamy. "A very special friend."

"You said you barely knew him," Reed reminded her caustically, "and then you said he was your roommate. Which is it going to be, Spring?"

Spring heard Mrs. K's little gasp and glared at Reed. "I never said he was my roommate! I started to say that he was my roommate's, er, brother when you rudely cut me off and jumped to your own conclusions. Well, Reed Caldwell, you can just keep jumping to all the conclusions you want because I have no intention of enlightening you about my relationship with Rob or anybody else!"

"I take it you have several of these relationships in your life?" he asked silkily, though his eyes were snapping with dangerous light.

"Yes, several!" she snapped back, and then felt disgusted. Considering what Reed believed the relationship to be, she didn't like the girl in the picture she was painting, and she detested lying. She always had.

What price am I asking myself to pay to buy protection from Reed's affection? she wondered wearily. Was the price her integrity, and was it worth it? No, one side of her said firmly, tell him the truth. But the other side held out for the wisdom of continuing to tell the kind of lies that would keep him angry and aloof. There was a price to be paid for allowing Reed to get close to her, and she had already paid it once.

She cast an embarrassed glance at Mrs. K and found that the old housekeeper, far from looking distressed, looked quite pleased about something.

"Now, now, you two," Mrs. K admonished mildly, putting a large pan of lasagna on the table, "I won't have quarrelling over dinner. Spring, I don't want to hear any more talk of leaving. You just got here, and I'm sure if you miss your special friend too much you could ask him to come here and see you, couldn't she Reed?"

Reed nearly choked on his lasagna. "I don't think you fully understand the nature of the relationship in question," Reed informed Mrs. K coldly, and Spring knew the subject was closed. Or would have been had Reed been dealing with anybody but Mrs. K.

"Nonsense," Mrs. K protested cheerfully. "I may not know Spring's young man, but I certainly know my Spring. What you're suggesting is ludicrous."

Ludicrous, Spring repeated smugly to herself, glaring balefully at Reed.

He ignored her, addressing Mrs. K with patience, though his irritation showed in a leaping muscle in his jaw. "Mrs. K, certain things have changed a great deal since you were Spring's age. I'm sure you'll find Spring quite, er, grown-up since she left here.''

"Grown-up?" Spring snorted rebelliously. "That's not the impression you gave me this morning when you were ordering me around like—"

"I used the term only in its most physical sense," Reed flung back tersely.

"Oh!" Spring exclaimed. "You vile, evil-minded—"

"Not over dinner," Mrs. K reminded her pleasantly. "More, Reed?"

He shook his head, glaring at Spring. She glared back defiantly.

Judd Black, the orchard foreman, chose that moment to make his entry. He was a big rawboned man about Reed's age with a thatch of unruly black hair, a homely face and friendly eyes. Judd had taken over Spring's father's job after his death, and he lived in one of the many rooms in the big house. They knew a little of each other from Mrs. K's letters, but Spring was not exactly feeling communicative and neither was Reed—a fact that seemed to bother neither Judd nor Mrs. K in the least. They chatted together happily, apparently oblivious to the strained silence between the other two at the table.

"I'm rather tired," Spring finally said weakly, at the exact moment Reed announced he had work to do in the orchard. They both said stiff good-nights to Mrs. K and Judd and went their separate ways.

"Tired!" Spring berated herself with exasperation. She had slept for seven hours in the car and wasn't used to sleeping at night anyway. She wished she had said that she was going for a walk, instead of trapping herself inside this room for the duration of the evening.

Especially this room. She glanced around it, unaware that her lips had a melancholy little twist to them. The room was a girl's room and wonderfully old-fashioned. It had lacy curtains at the window, a big four-poster bed and brightly polished hardwood floors. The quilt was predominantly pink and had been painstakingly hand done in a log-cabin pattern. Spring fingered it lovingly.

"This one," she could almost hear Reed's mother saying, "is from the baby blanket I once bought for the little girl we never had." Spring sighed. Dee had always wanted a little girl, had always wanted lots and lots of children, but it wasn't to be. There was only Reed....

Only Reed until the day he strolled in from the orchard with a rather grubby little elf attached to his hand.

"Her dad's one of the pickers," he explained nonchalantly. "He said it would be okay to give her some milk and cookies."

Spring became a regular for milk and cookies, initially shy and round eyed with wonder at the luxuries of the big house. But slowly the shyness dropped away, revealing a natural exuberance, warmth and lovingness.

Dierdre Caldwell started off by looking forward to the visits from her little friend. Soon she came to cherish them. Spring's mother, Dee discovered, had died very shortly after Spring was born. Her father was a big, laughing black Irishman, who worked hard when he worked and drank hard when he didn't. He loved Spring—braiding her hair each day with large, clumsy hands, making sure she was meticulously clean, reading her stories from worn books that he'd picked up cheap at secondhand stores. But all his love couldn't make up for the fact that he was a man and Spring's life was devoid of feminine touches. The suggestion of a pretty dress would have baffled him, and the complexities of registering his small daughter for school didn't mesh with his easygoing and transient life-style, so he'd simply never bothered. Dee found herself becoming increasingly concerned about the fate of her little visitor once picking season ended, and Spring's father, Ryan O'Hara, moved on.

"Bob," she addressed her husband one night over dinner, "it's time to expand."

Bob and Reed Caldwell regarded Dee with amazement. They had discussed expanding the orchard at some length, but Dee had been adamant that she saw little enough of her husband and son as it was.

Now, Dee, apparently blithely unaware she was reversing herself, continued casually. "Of course, you'd have to hire a foreman, especially with Reed starting university in the fall." She took a sudden interest in her plate. "What about Ryan O'Hara?"

"The man's a drunk!" Bob exclaimed. "And he doesn't know anything about orchards. He's a picker."

"He's not always drunk," Dee said, a betraying tremulous note entering her voice, "And he's very sharp. He'd learn. We could fix up the old log cabin out back for him . . . and Spring."

"Oh," Bob said with sudden understanding.

"And I could fix up a room for her here," Dee continued, allowing a trace of excitement to creep into her voice, "and then when he wanted to get away for a weekend—"

"You mean go on a tear," Bob interjected dryly.

"Bob—" it was little more than a whisper "—I love that little girl."

Bob sighed, then smiled tenderly at his wife of twenty years and covered her hand with his. "Kind of like her myself," he admitted gruffly.

Reed grinned and hopped up from his chair. "I'll go have a look at the cabin." He paused at the door and looked fondly back at his mother. "Wouldn't have been the same around here without her, would it?" he asked softly.

All day, Spring realized, she'd been fighting memories. Feeling something like relief, she gave up the fight, wandered over to the extrawide window ledge and sat down. She pulled up her legs, curled her arms around them and sighed. Let them come, she thought resignedly, let them come....

The little girl sat the big kitchen table, her long hair falling in a radiant wave to her waist. Suddenly a tall, strong-looking youth burst through the door, picked her up by her waist and swung her around and around over his head, filling the kitchen with her delighted shrieks.

Finally he put her back down in her chair and crouched in front of her, pushing a strand of her golden hair back from her flushed face.

"Know why your daddy called you Spring?" he asked softly.

"Why, Reed?" she whispered.

"Because it's snowing outside, but as soon as I see you I remember little blossoms peaking shyly out of their shells, the soft green grass, warm breezes and things that smell nice."

She giggled. He laughed. He was seventeen. She was seven. And her tiny heart nearly burst for loving him....

"Really for me?" she squealed, tumbling out of the cabin and stopping to stare with awe at the fat black-and-white pony Reed had on a rope.

"Happy birthday, sugar." He smiled and Spring darted by him, throwing her arms around the pony's sturdy neck and smothering it with kisses.

"You could say thank-you. It cost him nearly his whole summer's wages."

Spring noticed the lady for the first time and studied her without releasing her hold on the pony. Pretty, she thought, but with mean eyes. She scowled at Reed. "Who's she?"

"My girlfriend," Reed replied. He saw Spring's crestfallen expression and leaned close, whispering in her ear. "But not my best girl. Who's my best girl?"

Spring bit her lip and regarded him somberly. "Is it her birthday?"

"Eight years old today," he confirmed solemnly.

"That's me!" Spring crowed and sent the lady with the mean eyes a triumphant look....

"This is my very first dance, Reed." She wrapped her arms tighter around his neck. She decided it counted even if he had picked her up.

"You? A beautiful girl of ten?" he asked incredulously.

"Oh, I've been asked lots and lots. Even by Jimmy Allen, and Mary Louise says he's ever so handsome."

"So why didn't you say yes?"

She giggled and tilted back her head so that she could see his eyes. "Because, silly," she whispered, "he's not nearly so handsome as you."

Reed threw back his head and laughed. Spring smiled happily and burrowed her head back into the strong curve of his neck....

"Mary Louise, don't you think it's a little old? I'm only twelve."

Her friend thoughtfully regarded the fruit of her la-
bours—the hair was piled glamourously high on top of
Spring's head. "It's just right," she declared firmly.

Spring looked out the kitchen window of the cabin and
saw Reed crossing the yard. "I'll ask Reed. He'll know."
She dashed out after him.

"What do you think?" she asked, executing a perfect
little pirouette for him.

His lips twitched suspiciously, but he didn't laugh. "I
like it better than last week's," he finally said soberly.
"What was that? A French twist?"

"A French knot," she corrected him primly, and then
sighed. "You don't like it."

"It's a bit, er, old for you, sugar."

"How do you like my hair?" she persisted.

"Like this." He turned her around and patiently pulled
all the bobby pins out until her hair fell free, thick and
shining, to her waist. He turned her back around and
smiled. "Just like that."

"Mary Louise says it looks juvenile like this," Spring
protested.

"Just between you and me, Mary Louise knows nuts,"
Reed whispered conspiratorially....

"Reed?" she whispered brokenly into the darkness of
the barn. "Are you here?"

"I'm here," he answered just as brokenly, and she
followed his voice, finding him sitting on an overturned
apple bin, his head cradled in his hands.

"Daddy just told me about Bo and Dee's plane," she
choked.

He looked up at her, his face torn with anguish, and
then reached out and pulled her to him, cradling her head
against his chest and rocking her. Her hair became wet
with his tears.

"Reed, I'm so afraid. I never thought anything like this could happen to us. Not Bo and Dee... Reed, what if it never stops? What if you go away, too, and never come back?"

"I won't, sugar," he reassured her hoarsely.

"Promise," she insisted.

"I promise. You'll always have me. I promise," he soothed....

"Were you drinking last night?" he demanded coldly from behind his big desk.

"Reed, I'm fourteen years old!" she shouted.

"That doesn't answer my question."

Spring hesitated, then tossed her long, golden hair with defiance. "I had two beers."

"No dances for a month. And no horse for two weeks." He gestured dismissively at the door.

"You're not my father," she jeered.

"Too damned bad! If I was you'd get the licking you deserve. And if you back-talk me again, I'll give it to you anyway."

"You never used to be so mean," she observed angrily.

He only smiled. "You never used to be fourteen...."

A shiver of delight ran through Spring. Her father had shyly presented her with a dress of the palest yellow organza for her birthday, and she felt exquisitely grown-up. But Reed's present was even better. The living room of the big house had been transformed into a ballroom just for her, and now it was full of her friends who also looked surprisingly grown-up.

"May I have a dance with the loveliest lady here?" He said it somberly, and just as somberly she put her hand in his.

"So," he said, laughter creeping into the green of his eyes, "you've finally made it to sweet sixteen."

"And never been kissed," she murmured shyly, puzzled because she had never felt shy around Reed before.

"Not even by Jimmy Allen?" he teased. "God knows, he hangs around here enough."

Spring shook her head. "Not even by Jimmy Allen."

"Well, that won't do, will it?" He brushed his lips briefly and lightly across hers and laughed softly at the delicate blush that rose in her cheeks.

She hid her face against the solid wall of his chest. She had always loved Reed. Always. And yet something had just changed. Something she couldn't share with him, when she had always shared everything with him. She felt frightened by the vague sensation that his light kiss had aroused in her—frightened and exhilarated at the same time. She peeked up at his face, and her joyous feeling of being adult dissolved. She caught Reed winking with something less than brotherly interest at her teacher Miss Smith....

"Only six more months," Mary Louise announced with excitement, "and then we're free!"

Freedom obviously meant something different to each one of the girls scattered around Spring's bedroom in the big house, and soon their plans for the future were bouncing off the bedroom walls. Spring's room in the cabin wasn't big enough to allow her to take her turn at hosting the monthly hen party, but Reed always let her use this one, even if he did roll his eyes at the prospect of having eight high-spirited young women under his roof for the evening.

"What about you, Spring?"

"I haven't made any plans," she said too quickly, a blush rising in her cheeks.

Mary Louise looked at her shrewdly. "Out with it," she demanded.

The secret suddenly seemed too large and too exciting to keep to herself.

"I'm going to marry Reed," she responded softly.

The stunned silence that followed was finally broken by one small and awed question. "Has he asked you?"

Suddenly she felt only foolish and dreamy for having revealed her secret longing. "No," she admitted. Not only hadn't he asked, he didn't even know. She'd carefully hidden her feelings from him, along with the clamouring he'd caused in her heart since her sixteenth birthday.

Mary Louise snorted derisively. "Dare to dream," she snapped, and the other girls hooted.

"Ladies," the firm voice drifted down the hall, "would you kindly shut up? It's three o'clock in the morning."

"Who'd want him?" Sara whispered.

Me, Spring thought firmly, and she didn't join in the giggles....

It was a day only three weeks later when Spring awoke choking on smoke. Even in her panic, she knew what had happened. Dad had polished off the bottle of rye whiskey, tottered off to bed and lit a cigarette.

She raced, coughing violently, through the smoke-filled cabin to his room. She flung open the door, but a wall of flame met her.

"Daddy," she screamed, "Daddy!"

Suddenly strong arms wrapped around her. "Get out, Spring! The roof is going to go!"

"No!" She fought savagely against the arms around her, reaching for the flame, her eyes wild. "No!"

Reed picked her up, oblivious to her kicking and clawing, and raced out of the cabin with her. The roof gave one final creak and groan before caving in with a huge and ominous shower of sparks. . . .

There was something dreadfully wrong, Spring thought, as she entered Reed's office several weeks later. There was something in his face that was terrifying—a remoteness that made him a stranger before her eyes.

"Reed, what is it?" she whispered, unable to tear her eyes from that expression and feeling a crushing sense of foreboding.

"You can't stay here," he announced quietly. His voice, too, was that of a stranger. It had a steely edge to it that she'd never heard before.

"What do you mean?" Spring stammered, staring at his lean, suddenly hard profile with disbelief. "You're my guardian. It said so in the will."

"Spring, that means I have to do what I feel is best for you, no matter how hard that might be." His voice was frighteningly matter-of-fact.

"What are you talking about?" she cried shrilly, fear constricting her breathing.

He took a deep breath, his eyes lingering on her face with that unfamiliar and chilling expression in them. "There's a private school for girls in Victoria that I've looked into. I've got some leaflets you can look at. You're starting next week, Spring. In the fall I want you to go to college."

"No," she breathed, searching his face wildly, looking in that stony expression for even a flicker that would give her hope. "Why, Reed?" she finally whispered brokenly.

"Spring, I'm twenty-eight years old. I can't have an eighteen-year-old living under the same roof as me—not without starting some pretty ugly gossip."

"You never cared what people said about you before," she reminded him desperately.

"I don't give a damn what people say about me. I have a responsibility to you."

"But Mrs. K would be here. People would never think—"

"I have no intention of arguing with you about it, Spring," he snapped with bored impatience.

"But you can't do this! Haven't I lost enough already? I won't go away! I can go live with Mary—"

"Don't you think I've thought of every conceivable possibility?" he flashed angrily.

"Maybe not every one," she said slowly, her heart beginning to hammer with fear—and with elation—at what she was considering.

"Reed," she said, going around the desk to him and touching his shoulder beseechingly. "You could marry me," she whispered timidly.

His eyes met hers, and for a wild moment she thought a reprieve flashed through their depths. But a moment later she knew her imagination had been playing cruel tricks on her.

"That's out of the question," he growled, finality stamped into the glacial set of his features. "You're a child, Spring. Not much more than a baby. You don't even realize what you're talking about."

The Reed she knew had to be inside this cold stranger somewhere. She quelled the fear he was making her feel and impulsively reached out and ran her hand up the hard, muscular line of his chest.

"I'm not a child," she denied huskily. "I'll grow up. I promise, Reed. Don't send me away. Please."

He jerked away from her touch as though it had burned him and stood up. "I told you I've made up my mind," he bit out.

She stared at her feet and choked out the final admission that might save her. "I love you."

She peeked up at him through tear-encrusted lashes and inwardly recoiled from the look on his face. At most, she'd hoped her love would be returned. At least, that she would see his affection, his understanding, his sympathy.

But not a single emotion showed in his face—it was as hard and unyielding as granite. Without another word he turned from her, walked across the room and went out the door, shutting it quietly behind him.

She stared at the closed door for a long time, numb and stunned. He had said she was a child, and yet somehow she knew that childhood had just ended for her. The pain she felt was not a child's pain at all. It was the pain of a woman who had just discovered the deep, shattering, excruciatingly sad price of unrequited love.

Chapter Three

Spring's head flew up as she heard her bedroom door being opened, and she was suddenly aware of pain shooting through limbs that had been immobile for hours. Stiffly she unwrapped her arms from around her legs, stretched them and let them fall over the window ledge. All the while she watched Reed warily.

He stood leaning in the door stoop, shirtless and in bare feet, his arms folded over the rippling golden surface of his chest.

"I got up to get a glass of water," he explained quietly. "I saw the light under your door, and then I heard the oddest little sniffling noise." His voice was gently teasing, his eyes unmistakably concerned as they scanned her tear-stained face.

A shadow, she thought dully, of the Reed she had once known, the Reed who was so dangerous to her. But it's a lie, she screamed at herself desperately. The kindness you think you see in his eyes is hiding the horrible hardness of his heart, drawing you with its promise of warmth, only to impale you....

"What's the matter, Spring?" He came over to her on silent feet, pushed her over companionably and sat on the sill beside her, draping one arm easily over her shoulder.

She stiffened under his touch, noting the sudden quickening of her heart with frantic despair, willing herself to scream abuse at him or, at the very least, to jump up and walk away. But neither happened. Instead she found herself almost drugged by the scent of him—a heady masculine aroma of soap and sunshine, earth and apple blossoms. She heard something like a small mew of contentment emerge from her throat and felt her traitorous body cuddle in closer to the support of his arm and the broad expanse of his hard chest. Just for a moment, she told herself, I'll pretend just for a moment—

"Is it Rob?"

The words didn't register right away, just the deep comforting rumble of his voice within his chest.

Some small instinct for self-preservation reasserted itself. "Yes," she said shakily while her heart cried, "No!"

Reed sighed deeply and took her pointed little chin in his hand, forcing her to look into the clear, searching depths of his eyes.

"Spring, there are some things we should talk about." He let go of her chin, his eyes suddenly moody and turbulent as he studied a place on the wall across from them.

"I don't know you anymore, do I?" His question was musing and cut her to the quick. How could he not know her?

"You went away a shy and sheltered girl, and I guess I just thought you'd stay that way. I never gave you the skills to cope with the real world, so I had no right to be angry when you didn't cope." He stopped, still studying the wall, and then went on.

"And I was angry this morning, Spring, but I should've been angry with myself. I should've realized sooner that you'd be coming to maturity in a different age than mine, and you'd be facing problems and pressures far different from the ones I faced. It shouldn't have taken Rob strolling into your living room to so rudely awaken me." An unconscious scowl creased his brow.

"Reed," she pleaded, sensing the direction the conversation was moving in, "please don't say any more."

"Spring, I've avoided this responsibility for long enough, hoping that, magically, the new sexual mores weren't going to touch you. Thinking, for some stupid reason, that you just wouldn't get involved in the new age. Now I'm going to say the things you need to hear." He looked at her, the sternness back in his eyes. "And you're going to listen."

She wished he had the decency to look embarrassed or uncomfortable, but Reed looked like he took on the task of explaining sexual realities to naive young women every day.

"Spring, I'm not suggesting that clinging mindlessly to virginity is a virtue. I'm just trying to warn you that sex engaged in for sex's sake is a hollow, devastating experience. Especially for a woman. You see, intimacy, by its nature, creates bonding between people, powerful, magnificent bonding. It can make it seem like you're madly in love with a person you would be bored with if the relationship had been firmly grounded in areas like mutual tastes and interests, and plain old having things to talk about together. But everybody seems to be skipping the part about whether they genuinely like each other to get to the exciting part. But the exciting part is empty without love."

"Reed," she interjected weakly, "it's really a little late for the birds-and-the-bees talk."

He continued as if he hadn't heard her. "There's something else I want to say, Spring. You've always showed the promise of becoming a very attractive woman. Now you are. It must be a very heady, intoxicating experience for a young woman who has been rather isolated to be released on the world—to discover she wields a certain power over men. But that particular kind of power is fire, and if you play with it, you'll get burned."

"I don't know what you're talking about," she protested uncertainly.

He cocked a heavy brow at her. "I think you do."

"I don't," she snapped.

"I saw a glimmer of your knowing when you were eighteen. If you knew then, you know now."

She went crimson with rage. "You'd better explain yourself, Reed Caldwell!"

"All right," he agreed coolly. "You knew then that a certain kind of touch, a certain look, a certain tone of voice, made a promise, the kind of a promise that can bring a man to his knees. But I don't think you knew then exactly what you were promising. I wonder if you do now."

Spring closed her eyes, suddenly sickened, remembering her hand caressing his chest that night he had told her he was going to send her away. Part child, part woman. Had she known? Yes, she admitted slowly, some secret, almost instinctive side of herself had known just what she was offering him that night. But it hadn't been a cheap gesture, an act of prostitution, as he was insinuating. It had been the awakening of a child into a woman, it had been the offering of a gift. How could he believe she would ever offer that to anyone else?

"Rob said he was going to marry you, Spring," Reed continued dispassionately. "I didn't believe him, and if you did, you were a fool. Men are sometimes ruled by a darker side."

So that was it, she thought, not thrilled with her enlightenment. Reed thought she was pining away the night, weeping for a man she had enticed into bed in exchange for a marriage proposal. He was trying to tell her the power he thought she wielded over men would be meaningless in the light of day. And he thinks I'm the fool, she thought distractedly. He must know me better than that. He must... But by his own admission he'd said he didn't know her anymore, she concluded wearily.

"It's been a very informative little session," she managed with some sarcasm, pushing herself away from the compelling warmth of his body. "But if you're quite finished, I'm tired."

He watched her, his eyes coldly assessing, as if he wondered how much of what he'd said had registered with her.

Let him wonder, she thought savagely. I wouldn't give him the satisfaction of knowing his first instinct—that somehow the sexual revolution would pass me by—was entirely correct.

He'd gotten up from the window and stood at the door. She glanced at him, and her resolve almost died. Reed's eyes, of late so expressionless and devoid of emotion, had something in them that almost made her gasp with dismay. It was sadness. A lingering, overwhelming sadness. For a moment she almost went to him. She even pictured herself laying her hand on his forearm, looking up into his eyes and telling him the truth.

Telling him that he hadn't told her anything she didn't already believe. That long ago she'd reached the conclusion that sex without love would be a travesty. How could that surprise him, when she'd grown up in his shadow, looking to him for her example? She'd learned values in part from him, but her ideals also sprang from deep within her. Her beliefs about love and sex were instinctive.

"Good night, Spring." He was gone before her internal debate was finished.

Why the sadness? she wondered, looking at the place he had stood. Because he believed he had failed her, or because he believed she had failed him? Or was it the sadness of an older brother looking at the sister he'd teased, played with and helped to grow up, only to realize that by helping her, he would lose her?

An older brother? Spring questioned herself. No, she hadn't thought of Reed as an older brother in a long, long time. Even before she'd turned sixteen he'd been her whole world. She'd had her first crush on him, and the feeling hadn't dwindled and died as crushes were supposed to. Instead her affection had matured and grown deeper. Yet, if she were going to be brutally realistic, he'd never once treated her as anything but a kid sister.

Why had Reed insisted she come home? And why had she agreed? She had agreed, really. He hadn't forced her, he'd only made it easy for her to do what she really wanted to do.

Does he love me? She frowned. A dangerous thought. And would a man who loved her give the kind of advice he had just given her? Or practically accuse her of prostitution? she reminded herself grimly. She didn't think so, unless he loved her in completely the wrong way, an older brother keeping a stern and benevolent eye on her life.

And what of you, Spring? a small, persistent voice asked her. *What do you feel for him?* Nothing, she thought vehemently. Oh, she didn't deny that she had once, but she was older now and hopefully wiser. She knew the price of caring for a man like Reed.

Ah, the little voice teased, *that may be so, but do you really think love is something you can turn on and off like a water faucet?*

I hate him, Spring told herself firmly. But the little voice got in one more shot. *So, it is not 'nothing' that you feel. And what is hate,* it asked her, *but the flip side of love? Not to love is to feel indifference. To hate is to admit that another still holds some mysterious power over you. Love and hate are not so different as they first appear. They well up from the same source—* Spring shut off the little voice with impatient abruptness, put on her nightgown and went to bed. Sleep was very nearly instant.

Spring had expected to feel exhausted the next day. Instead she awoke early, feeling buoyant. It was the sun, she told herself, stretching like a cat—the sun, the birds chirping merrily outside her window and the faint smell of apple blossoms. It was so different from the grey gloom of her room in Vancouver and the never ending noises from the street and neighbouring apartments. She allowed herself to stay in bed for a little while, just relishing the brilliance of her sun-drenched room.

Then she bounced out of bed and pawed through her suitcase looking for something to wear. Her wardrobe was still dominated by the jeans and T-shirts that had been the dress of the day at college and that her salary at Cap's wouldn't have allowed her to replace even if she had wanted to. Undaunted by the lack of choice, she put on a pair of jeans and a rather wrinkled but very colourful Hawaiian shirt that matched her mood. She threw open her window, decided the day promised to be hot and carelessly coiled her hair into a knot at the top of her head. After studying herself, she pulled down a few wisps of curling hair to frame her face.

She scampered down the wide staircase, running her fingers down the lovely wood of the banister, barely able to contain a grin. Why do I feel so wonderful? she asked herself. How long has it been since I felt eager to see how the day would unfold? A long time, she answered herself, a very long time. And who cared about stuffy old Reed or his lectures on morality? She decided to just stay out of his way and enjoy feeling good while it lasted. And she certainly didn't ask herself if "stuffy old Reed" could in any way be responsible for the good feeling springing up so spontaneously from within her.

"Good morning, Mrs. K. Isn't it a lovely day?"

Mrs. K turned from the bread she was kneading at the counter and smiled at her. "Oh, not bad for a lazy little backwater," she teased dryly, and then studied Spring with appreciation. "My goodness, this country air has you looking better already. Now—" she turned to the fridge "—let's see what a good country breakfast can do. Bacon, eggs, pancakes, orange juice . . ."

Spring laughed. "I don't want to offend you, but a cup of coffee would suit me fine. I'm sorry, Mrs. K, but I've gotten out of the habit of eating breakfast."

"Humph! Most important meal of the day. No wonder you don't look healthy. But I've got just the thing," she muttered with a satisfied gleam in her eyes. "Just the thing." A few minutes later she placed a heaping bowl of strawberries, generously smothered in heavy cream, in front of Spring.

"Tell me you can't eat that," she challenged, folding her angular arms over her chest.

"You win. I can eat strawberries and cream anytime."

"Me, too," Reed said, coming in the door.

"You're having bacon and eggs," Mrs. K informed him. "I'm not sending you out to do a hard day's work on strawberries."

Reed sat down across from Spring and winked at her. She couldn't contain her smile at his boyish expression. How different he seemed from the stern, intimidating man who had appeared on her doorstep yesterday morning. Only yesterday, she thought, and yet suddenly it seemed like she had never gone away, especially with Reed seeming so much the way he had once been.

"I'm having strawberries and cream," he insisted stubbornly, and then glanced over his shoulder at Mrs. K's formidable expression. "Okay," he conceded, "I'll have strawberries and cream first, and then I'll have bacon and eggs."

"You can't eat bacon and eggs after strawberries and cream," Mrs. K informed him with a sniff. "It'll ruin your taste buds."

"I can and I will," Reed replied with mock severity, "and you remember who fastens his name to the paycheques around here."

Mrs. K sniffed again, but there was a hint of a smile on her lips when she set a huge bowl of strawberries in front of him. "Don't make it a habit," she warned. "Now, what are you doing today?"

"Mowing. We've got a bumper crop of dandelions this year, and the bees seem to think they get paid to pollinate those damn things instead of the blossoms. What are you going to be up to, Spring?''

"I thought I'd saddle up Stormy and take her for a ride. I hope I still know how to ride!''

There was an awkward silence in the kitchen, and Spring didn't miss the look exchanged between Reed and Mrs. K.

"Stormy's gone,'' Reed finally said quietly, pushing the strawberries away, his face once again hard and stern, and not at all boyish.

"Gone?'' Spring whispered. A picture of her dancing dapple-grey Arabian mare flashed through her mind. Those huge, soulful eyes, the velvet of her nose. "She's not dead, is she?'' Spring forced herself to ask.

Reed looked grim. "No, she's not dead.'' He hesitated. "I gave her away.'' His voice was soft but not apologetic.

Spring stared at him disbelievingly. "How could you?'' she finally grated accusingly. In a flash they were strangers again, and she angrily quelled her momentary regret.

He sighed. "Spring, she needed attention. She was getting fat. I just didn't have the time to exercise her every day.''

"Oh right!'' Spring spat out disdainfully. "I almost forgot what an important man you are. The high and mighty orchardist! You wouldn't have half an hour a day to spend with a mere horse, would you, Reed? Or to find some poor kid who was dying to ride to come out and exercise her? No, that's not your style at all. Your style is just to get rid of things that cause problems, that don't fit in with your picture of perfection. Horses. People. If they're too much trouble, out they go. No alternatives, no discussions, just what Reed Caldwell wants and to hell with who gets trampled or hurt along the way—''

"Shut up!" he snapped, his eyes furious, white lines of strain showing around his mouth. He stood up and towered over her, his face dark, savage and frightening. For a moment she felt certain he was going to reach across the distance that separated them and slap her. But the fury faded from his features, and suddenly he only looked tired. He shoved his clenched fists deep in his pockets, spun on his heel and strode out the door.

"Oh, Spring," Mrs. K sighed reproachfully.

"I don't care," Spring said defiantly. "It's true."

"No, it's not, love. Try not to be so hard on Reed."

"How can you defend him?" Spring demanded. "He gave away *my* horse. That's just mean, nothing else."

"He gave away Stormy because she was breaking his heart!" Mrs. K snapped, and then looked sorry.

"Ha! He doesn't have a heart to break." But Spring was looking at Mrs. K curiously. "What do you mean?"

"Spring, she used to stand at the fence and wait for you to come home from school. She'd wait for hours, her head drooping lower and lower when you didn't come. I used to see Reed standing at the edge of the orchard watching her, and I swear he looked as beaten as she did. One day he just came in and said he decided to give her away. I was glad, and you should be, too. She was your pet, Spring, and the only thing to do was find another little girl who could lavish her with love and attention."

"Who'd he give her to?" Spring asked in a low voice, staring at her hands.

"A beautiful little Indian girl—with huge black eyes."

Spring's head flew up at Mrs. K's tone, but Mrs. K turned hastily away from her. "I've already said more than I should have. This is between him and you, after all." She sighed. "I'm turning into a foolish old woman. Now, eat up and clear out of my kitchen. I've got bread to finish."

Spring ate her strawberries in confused silence. Mrs. K tended to worship Reed; he could do no wrong in her eyes. But still, Stormy *had* always waited by the fence when she got off the school bus. Even when she was late, Stormy was there, waiting patiently and nickering a soft greeting. But Reed's heart breaking over it? Ha! And what was the significance of Reed having given the horse to a little girl with big black eyes?

Her inner contentment of earlier shattered, Spring deposited her bowl in the sink and, feeling deeply troubled, wandered outside. The implications of what Mrs. K had said were overwhelming. That would mean that Reed felt something stronger than what he'd ever let on. And yet to believe it, even to hope for it, was to leave herself wide open to being hurt again, to being disappointed by him again, to finding out he didn't feel quite the way she wanted.

So what do I do? she wondered, digging a little hole in the garden with the toe of her sneaker. It was not as if he'd given her a single reason to think he thought anything about her at all. But she decided to wait. To do nothing but *wait* and see if Reed would reveal his hand. And until then?

The garden suddenly came into focus in front of her, and she noticed that it looked sadly neglected. Then she remembered that Mrs. K had written and said she was getting too old to garden, that weeding in the intense summer heat made her feel much older than her sixty-two years.

Spring dropped to her knees and picked up a handful of the rick black soil, held it to her nose and breathed in the earthy, good scent of it. Yes, she would wait—and plant the garden.

Spring huffed and puffed behind the Rototiller, stopping to wipe the sweat out of her eyes. It felt good to be working so hard. This was her second day struggling behind the unwieldy machine, and last night she'd fallen into bed too exhausted to think, every muscle in her body aching. But it was a pleasant ache, and she decided she'd rather spend the rest of her life pushing a Rototiller than ever spend another hour in a place like Cap's Café.

She saw Reed coming up from the orchard, and she brought her break to a hasty close. Although she appeared to be ignoring him, she was in fact incredibly aware that he'd stopped to watch her with amused eyes.

Suddenly he was beside her, switching the machine off. "Time for lunch," he told her when the noise had died away. He frowned. "Where's your hat? I told you to wear a hat until you got more accustomed to the sun."

Her hand went to her head, and sure enough she found it bare and very hot. She glanced around the garden, but Reed spotted the hat first, lying behind her in one of her rather crooked furrows. He picked it up and plunked it on her head, pushing it down almost to her nose.

"Are you sure you don't want me to do this for you?" he asked, studying her furrows, and then he looked at her with a small smile. She looked hastily away from him. Darn, but he looked appealing when those white teeth flashed against the deep bronze of his skin.

"I want to do it myself," she insisted stubbornly.

His smile widened, and he shrugged. "Okay."

She became aware that the tension, forever present between them, was momentarily gone, and hesitating for only a second, she decided to take advantage of it.

"Reed, I'm sorry I said some of the things I said the other day when you told me about Stormy."

His green eyes held hers searchingly. "Only some of the things?" he queried softly.

She bit her lip angrily. *Damn him! Does he have to make it so hard? What does he want?* Well, if he wanted her to say he'd been right to send her away, he was going to have one long wait, in fact, hell could freeze over first!

"Yes," she snapped, pushing the hat up on her brow, barely noticing when it toppled off again.

He bent slowly, scooped it up and wordlessly settled it back on her head. He made her feel like a difficult but not unmanageable child.

"Well, what do you want?" she demanded.

"I want you to—" He stopped, and the fleeting wistful expression vanished from his eyes. "Never mind. Forget it." He turned his back indifferently to her and walked up to the house.

She squinted after him somberly. She knew intuitively how that line would have ended. She knew he wanted her to say she forgave him. But why couldn't he ask? Because he didn't believe he'd done anything to be forgiven for? Or because he knew that she couldn't forgive him for *that*?

Remembering she'd initially planned some kind of truce, she muttered, "I don't think I'm cut out for diplomacy," threw down her gloves and followed him to the house.

It seemed, over the next few days, that she would prove herself right on the diplomacy count. Anytime she and Reed spoke to one another, the sparks flew and fights erupted, often over the most ridiculous things. They argued whether or not to plant zucchini—he hated it— whether she should take over the rather extensive paperwork for the orchard—she told him bluntly he was making a mess of it—and whether he or Judd should take on the task of teaching her to drive. He won out on not planting zucchini, and she won on doing the paperwork and having Judd teach her to drive.

And despite the friction she couldn't help but notice she felt content with life. She woke up in the mornings eager to be up and about, and each day seemed full to bursting. She caught herself wandering around humming merry little tunes and singing loudly and unselfconsciously as she worked in her garden. She was getting a tan, gaining weight, and she noticed she was laughing easily and often. And something was changing between her and Reed, too. Oh, the friction was there, but there was also a comfort with each other that she couldn't quite explain.

I'm happy, she thought, sticking her finger in the dirt and dropping a carrot seed into the hole. *I don't even know why. I just am.*

Out of the corner of her eye she saw Reed walking by the garden with a haughty expression on his face. He was still miffed, she assumed, because she'd told him this morning that she could never learn to drive with him sitting beside her shouting in her ear.

"Damn it, Spring, I don't shout at you," he'd shouted, then stopped, glowered at her and stalked from the room. A little while later Judd had come up to the house and asked her shyly when she would like her first lesson.

Mischievously Spring picked up a clod of dirt and winged it at Reed. She gave a little gasp when it hit him square in the chest, and then seeing the look on his face, she giggled, jumped up and ran. She went over the garden fence like a young deer and bounded out into the orchard.

She could hear his feet pounding along the ground behind her and was now laughing so hard she could barely run, not that she could have outrun him anyway. He was so close that she could feel his breath on her neck, and then suddenly his arms went around her waist, and they both tumbled to the ground.

"You're squishing me," she gasped.

He rolled off her, but not before he'd snared her wrist and pulled her, none to gently, to her feet.

"What do I do now?" he asked with sternness that didn't fool her because she could see the laughter in his eyes. "Spank you or kiss you?"

"I'm too old to be spanked," she said, trying vainly to twist out of his grasp.

"Yes," he agreed softly. "You are." And suddenly the laughter was gone from his eyes, and she became very still. He reached out with his free hand and brushed some dirt from her face, his hand lingering on her cheek.

His eyes were very dark all of a sudden, and she found them dangerously sensuous, especially framed with the dark, thick tangle of lashes. She tried to flee the captivity of his eyes, but her gaze moved on to even more captivating territory, exploring the firm set of his lips with an aching hunger. Hardly knowing what she was doing, she reached up with her free hand and traced the line of his lower lip, feeling a shiver move from her fingertips to tingle tantalizingly along her spine.

He released her wrist, placing strong hands on the flat of her back and compelling her toward him, closer and closer until finally their bodies touched. She stiffened, startled by the current that jolted through her, and then felt herself melting into the warmth of his body, becoming so close that she didn't know where he ended and she began.

Sensation after sensation swept her as they stood locked together—the feel of the curling hairs on his chest against her chin; the searing heat of his hands on her back; the taut muscle of his thigh where it pressed hers; his strong, clean scent overpowering even the blossoms. She dared not move, lest anything change, and the perfection of this moment be lost.

His hand came to her chin and lifted it. His darkened eyes scanned her face. And then slowly his lips came down and claimed hers, gently and tenderly. It was as if, despite all he'd accused her of, he knew somehow that this was the first time she'd been kissed—truly kissed, as a woman by a man.

She met his kiss shyly, fleetingly self-conscious and worried about what she was expected to do. And then a new kind of knowledge opened up to her, and without thinking she knew exactly what to do next. Her lips parted, and his tongue caressed them, then moved with breathtaking intensity into the inviting hollow of her mouth.

Her heart pounded with the savagery of a storm-tossed surf, and quaking began deep within her. It was every sensation she'd ever known—fireworks and roller coasters—all wrapped into one. It was an intoxicating journey into the unknown, and its path threatened to unleash an inferno of passion within her.

Finally his lips left her mouth, and the storm slowly gave way to a tranquil calm. He continued to hold her close, one hand stroking the silk of her hair as gently and as lightly as one would stroke a hummingbird's wings.

At last she tilted back her head and looked at him.

"Welcome home, Spring," he said quietly, then smiled and kissed away the single joyous tear that slipped down her cheek.

Chapter Four

Spring suspected she was going to be kissed once again, well and thoroughly. More instinctively than provocatively, her lips parted slightly in anticipation.

"Reed? Reed, darling, where are you?"

Spring found herself abruptly released from the comforting warmth of Reed's embrace as he turned toward the sound of that husky, feminine voice.

"Down here," he called cheerfully through the rows of trees.

Spring, too, turned toward the source of the call, and she could barely contain a gasp when the woman appeared. She was, without a doubt, the most beautiful woman Spring had ever seen.

She was strikingly tall and built like a model, slim and yet attractively proportioned. Her heavy mane of red-gold hair fell past her shoulders and had a carefully contrived wildness to it. Her facial features and complexion were perfect, and she used only the faintest brush of makeup. Her eyes were huge, a soft suede brown, flecked with gold and rimmed by natural, ridiculously long lashes.

She was dressed in what Spring gauged to be a very expensive taupe-coloured silk suit, which looked disgustingly sexy despite its straight lines. She was also wearing ridiculously high spike-heel shoes, and Spring noticed with some satisfaction that she was having trouble balancing on the uneven ground.

Her satisfaction died when the woman reached them and fastened herself to Reed's arm for support. "Darn shoes," she said with a rueful grin.

"Spring," Reed said turning to her, "this is my friend, Penny Bryer."

Penny smiled up at him and scrunched up her nose. "Really," she said softly, "sometimes 'friend' is such an inadequate word." She turned her attention to Spring, and Spring was a little disconcerted by the genuine warmth in her eyes. There was no high-fashion hauteur here; the eyes sparkled with friendly openness and a trace of mischievousness.

"Spring," she said in her husky voice, studying her with interest. "My God, but you're beautiful! That combination is absolutely exotic. Your hair, and those eyes. And a tan! I think I could hate you," she teased lightly. "People with your colouring are supposed to burn red as beets just like I do."

"I never burn," Spring said stiffly.

"Lucky you," Penny said, apparently not noticing the stiffness. "Mrs. K sent me out to find you two. Lunch is getting cold. She asked me over to meet Spring." Penny winked widely at Reed, leaving no doubt in Spring's mind that meeting her had not been the attraction at all. "Now, Reed, lend me your arm. These shoes are impossible.

Cute, but impossible. Are your confounded trees stuffing yet?''

Reed laughed. "It's called petal sluff when the blooms start to fall . . . and yes, they are. And if you want to win the heart of a man who earns his living from apples, you never refer to them as those confounded trees. Never.''

Spring's face froze. "If you want to win the heart of a man," she repeated slowly. Oh God, she thought wildly, she let him do it again. She let him worm his way into her heart only to betray her. *How could you, Reed?* she silently asked the broad back in front of her, noting dejectedly that his and Penny's heads were close together, and that she was murmuring to him confidentially. "'Friend' is such an inadequate word," Spring recalled Penny saying, and felt something inside her die a torturous death.

Over lunch she watched Penny with dull agony. The other woman in the storybooks was always so wicked and hateful and phony, but Penny wasn't. She was vivacious, articulate and fun. She also vaguely reminded Spring of someone, though for the life of her, she couldn't pinpoint who. Penny was obviously a frequent guest, and both Mrs. K and Judd, as well as Reed, seemed to delight in her company. Well, not me, Spring thought grimly, I hate her.

"Spring," Penny addressed her, "Mrs. K told me you wanted her to drive you downtown this afternoon to pick up some shorts and sunsuits. I was going shopping anyway, and it's so much more fun to have another woman along. Let's go together."

Spring was briefly startled that the older girl saw her as a woman, although *not* as competition, she told herself ruefully. "I'm sorry," Spring said coolly. "I can't. I have to—''

"Nonsense," Mrs. K said, cutting her off. "You've been after me for two days to take you into town. Go while you have the chance."

Without actually screaming that she hated Penny Bryer with all her heart and soul, Spring couldn't think of a way to get out of this, so half an hour later she was seated in a baby-blue Trans Am beside Penny.

Does this woman ever stop talking? Spring asked herself waspishly, only half-listening to a conversation peppered with Mrs. K this and Judd that, and Reed... Spring let herself drift into her own thoughts, not listening to Penny at all.

"I love that man!" Penny exclaimed, slamming a well-manicured fist into the steering wheel for emphasis, and Spring was drawn abruptly from her tortured introspection.

"I've been chasing him for two years, casting my pride to the winds, and I don't even think he knows I'm alive."

"I think he knows you're alive," Spring offered without enthusiasm.

"Do you?" Penny asked eagerly. "But do you think he knows how I feel about him?"

"Sure...I certainly did." If there was mild sarcasm in Spring's tone, Penny didn't seem to notice.

"Did you?" Penny laughed with a girlish little tinkle.

"Yes," Spring said flatly.

"But then why doesn't he respond? Do you think it's because of my money? He's so awfully proud. But damn, what would he have me do? Stand on street corners and give the stuff away?" She scowled thoughtfully. "Maybe it's not the money at all. Maybe it's because I'm divorced. Oh, I hate the stereotype of divorced women! I'm not hard or loose, or predatory. I just got married too young, to a nincompoop who was determined to drink himself into an early grave. Surely I'm allowed one mistake. But then he's so stupidly old-fashioned at times, isn't he?"

"Yes," Spring agreed wholeheartedly. "Look," she added curtly and cruelly, "maybe he just doesn't love you."

"Yes," Penny agreed with a soulful sigh, "maybe that is it. And you can't force people to love you, can you?"

"No," Spring concurred, with her first trace of genuine sympathy. "No, you can't force people to love you."

"But, Spring, if I *really* thought he didn't, I would have given up long before now. But sometimes I see the way he looks at me, and I just know. He's been a bachelor too long. That's the problem. It's become a comfortable habit, and he's scared to death to try anything else."

Penny's pretty jaw set stubbornly. "I think it's time to haul out the big guns. Plan B, so to speak." She sighed. "If Reed would just cooperate the tiniest little bit, I'd have him eating out of the palm of my hand in no time."

The idea of Reed eating out of the palm of anybody's hand struck Spring as being so ludicrous she almost snorted, but then she looked again into that stunningly beautiful face.

"Oh, let's forget it," Penny suggested as they turned into Vernon's city centre. "I love this downtown. It's got so much charm and character. Don't you think so, Spring?"

Spring's eyes roamed affectionately over the small downtown area. The sidewalks were cobblestoned and lined with trees in planters. Comfortable wooden benches sat under them. Most of the buildings were old with modern facades.

"It's all right," Spring said blandly, believing that the less Penny thought they had in common, the better.

"Would you have rather gone to the mall?" Penny asked anxiously.

"No," Spring said hastily and got out of the car.

Penny, she realized reluctantly, *was* fun to shop with. She had an unerring eye for colour and fashion, and she picked outfits for Spring to try on that Spring realized were far more flattering to her than anything she would have picked for herself.

"Spring, you've got to take those black silky shorts and the white top with the string straps."

For the first time, Spring hesitated. "Aren't they a bit . . . sleazy?"

Penny laughed. "Spring, darling, you couldn't look sleazy if you walked down Main Street in your birthday suit. You have a wonderful quality about you, especially in your eyes. It's almost haunting, it's so innocent and lovely."

Damn, Spring thought, I have to get away from this woman. I'm actually starting to like her despite myself.

"That's it," she said after she'd purchased the black shorts and the top. "I've gone overboard already, and I'm tired of shopping."

"Oh, good," said Penny. "Let's do the really fun part now. We'll find a coffee shop and gorge on something disgustingly sweet and fattening. I want to pick up a few things, and then I'll take you back."

But Spring wanted desperately to get away from Penny. At the moment she felt a reluctant affection for her, which she most certainly did not want to feel.

"Penny, would you mind if I ran over to the library while you went for coffee? There's a couple of books on gardening that I want to have a quick peek at." She felt ridiculously guilty for the lie, but Penny shrugged good-naturedly.

"I should come, too, and check out some books on orchards so that at least I know what I'm competing against, but—" she shrugged "—I don't like to read. Maybe I can get you to explain it all to me sometime."

Spring left her and turned off Main Street to walk the two short blocks to the library. She didn't even go inside but plunked herself down on the low wall that surrounded the gurgling fountain and watched it grimly. A rather tame mallard swam up to her and gazed at her hopefully, but she didn't even notice.

How can he resist her? she wondered sadly. I can barely resist her, and I *want* to hate her. Penny was puzzling. She told Spring that she was beautiful, and helped her pick gorgeous clothes, yet when she talked of the competition, she talked of an orchard. Maybe she's more sure of Reed than she lets on, Spring thought woefully, or maybe she knows there isn't a woman alive who could compete with her.

Life was so unfair. How could a woman be born as perfect as Penny? It was an uneven distribution of assets that one woman had so much—brains, beauty, wit, charm, vitality—

"Hello."

Spring looked up at the man who stood gazing down at her with a small, tentative smile playing across his lips.

"Hi," she returned, but without encouragement.

"May I join you?"

She wanted to tell him to get lost, that she was busy, but she couldn't bring herself to be that insensitive. He had nice eyes she thought absently, very large and hazel. Actually, she noted without much interest, he was very nice looking. His head was covered with a thick crop of black curls, and he was tall and broad across his shoulders—though not as tall or broad as Reed. She guessed him to be close to her own age.

"I'm Réjean Brassard," he introduced himself, and she noticed the thick, pleasant French accent for the first time. "And you?"

"Spring O'Hara."

He cocked his head at her. "For true?"

"Pardon?"

"Is that your real name?"

"Of course," she said sourly.

He smiled, and she forgave him, because he really had a very pleasant smile. "It suits you very much."

"Thank you," she said awkwardly, wishing he'd go away because she didn't know what to say to him. She needn't have worried.

He led the conversation skillfully, asking her questions and delighting her, despite herself, with an outrageous sense of humour.

"Where do you live?" he asked.

"On an orchard in the Coldstream," she told him.

"Ah, the orchards," he responded. "That's why I first came to this area. I wanted to see Canada, and the French-speaking radio stations in Quebec were advertising for pickers out west." He grinned without embarrassment. "It turned out to be the perfect job for me. I pick for a few months of the year and collect unemployment insurance for the rest of it."

Spring could almost see Reed's disapproval, and she had to admit that she didn't exactly feel approving herself. She glanced at the huge tower clock next to the fountain and rose. "I really must go. I have to meet a friend."

"Wait. Don't go yet. I'd like to see you again. Maybe I could take you to a movie this weekend."

"Oh, no. I don't think so."

His handsome features looked suddenly harsh. "Is it because I'm a Frenchman?"

Spring was dimly aware that there was a certain undeserved prejudice against French Canadians in the valley, and she felt absurdly responsible for it at the moment. "Of course it's not that," she stammered.

"Ah, a formidable father, then?"

"I don't live with my father. He's dead. I live with—" Spring stopped, suddenly uncertain what to say. She couldn't very well say that she lived with a man she wasn't related to. It could be misconstrued, would be misconstrued in this age of casual relationships. "With my uncle," she finished weakly.

"And he is formidable?" Réjean pressed.

Spring grinned. "You might say that."

"Tell you what. I'll give you my phone number, and if you change your mind about the movie, give me a call." He gave her an engaging smile. "And I'm very good with formidable fathers... and uncles."

She took his phone number, more not to hurt his feelings than because she had any intention of ever calling him. She waved casually over her shoulder and went off in search of Penny.

"What do you think of plan B?" Penny asked her, whipping a lovely frothy violet-coloured dress out of the box beside her on the car seat. "Of course, this is only a minor part of it."

Spring looked at the dress and felt her heart sink. It was gorgeous. It didn't take much imagination to know how the dress would cling to Penny's trim figure and how its plunging neckline would draw the eye. The dress was definitely "the kind of promise that brings a man to his knees," and Spring instinctively knew that it would take one hell of a man to resist that particular promise.

"It's nice," she said coldly, with deliberate understatement.

"Nice? It's naughty as hell," Penny said, looking at Spring thoughtfully. "You don't like me. Do you, Spring?"

Spring was caught off guard by the unexpected bluntness of the question and felt herself blushing uncomfortably under Penny's steady gaze. "I really don't know you well enough to say," she hedged.

Penny sighed. "I'm almost uncannily perceptive about how people feel, Spring. But I guess I kind of overwhelm people sometimes, and they don't know how to take me. I hope you'll like me when you get to know me better."

"Why?"

"Oh, can't you guess?" Penny asked with gentle exasperation. "If things work out the way I'd like them to, you and I are going to be practically living on top of one another. I was hoping we could feel really good about each other, almost like sisters."

She wants me to like her because she knows how responsible Reed feels for me, Spring deduced blackly. She thinks if she can win me over, he'll come to heel that much more easily. If we liked each other and got along famously, he wouldn't feel like he had to kick me out again, in order to marry her.

Could he marry her? Spring thought bleakly. But of course that's what Penny was aiming for, and of course that's why she had made the reference to a sisterly relationship. But I can't picture Reed married, she wanted to wail childishly. Except that she could—but not to Penny Bryer.

Well, Penny, she thought, you needn't worry. If he marries you I certainly won't stick around. We'll never be living "practically on top of one another." You don't seem to understand at all how I feel about him. If you love him, how could you miss that? Are you that sure of yourself?

"Spring, I'm sorry. Now I've upset you. When will I learn not to jump all over people as if I'd known them all my life?"

She is perceptive, Spring thought, and she was obviously genuinely concerned. She made an effort to smile at Penny. "I'm not upset. And who knows," she forced herself to say, "perhaps we will feel sisterly toward one another someday." Over my dead body, she added to herself, looking determinedly out the window.

The trip home passed in rather strained silence until Penny suddenly pulled off the gravel road. "There's Reed," she said eagerly, and honked the horn to get his attention.

He was shirtless, standing beside a tractor, his muscles rippling with strain as he wrestled with some mysterious part of the tractor engine. Spring's stomach did an odd little flip-flop at the sight of his broad, naked back, and she remembered the taste of his lips on hers this morning with something close to agony.

He glanced at them, grinned to acknowledge he knew they were there and then threw his weight behind the wrench. A moment later he tossed down the tool with satisfaction and picked up his shirt. He came over to the car, wiping his hands carelessly on the shirt.

"Have a good afternoon?" he asked, leaning his strong brown arms on the window ledge of Spring's door.

He was so close, Spring could smell the faintly spicy and entirely pleasant aroma of his sweat. She refused to meet his eyes, looking stubbornly straight ahead.

"Reed." Penny leaned forward to see around Spring. "Did you decide about Saturday night? Please say you'll come. I bought a new dress just for the occasion."

One of his strong hands had found its way to Spring's hair, and he absently twisted a golden strand around his fingers. "Penny, I told you I don't want to go all the way to Kelowna. And I sure as hell don't want to wear a tux in this heat. I kind of thought I might build a bonfire in the yard pit Saturday night and sit around with my best girl roasting hot dogs and eating marshmallows." He had tugged Spring's hair gently when he said 'best girl,' and she stiffened with confused discomfort.

He was using her! Spring surmised angrily. Using her to make Penny jealous. Penny was his for the asking. Why would he be toying with her? Oh, but wasn't that Reed's style? To keep everybody guessing, to manipulate and control everything and everyone around him? Despicable, despicable, man!

Penny didn't seem the least put out. "All the way to Kelowna? Reed, it's half an hour away! My car's got air-conditioning if yours doesn't, so you needn't worry about being too uncomfortable in your tux. And Spring won't mind if I borrow you for the evening, will you, Spring?"

I don't believe these two, Spring thought wildly. "For heaven's sake, I don't own Reed," she snapped, "and Reed, it's very kind of you to appoint yourself to my entertainment committee, but I've already made plans for Saturday night."

She could feel his curious gaze burning into her skin, but she took sudden interest in the packages on her lap, so that she didn't have to meet that gaze.

"Come on, Reed," Penny said, her large eyes round and pleading.

Reed laughed. "You're spoiled rotten, Penny. Do you always get your way?"

Penny grinned. "Nearly always. Pick me up around eight, love?"

He nodded and rose from his leaning position, touching Spring's arm. "I'll talk to you later," he said in a low growl, that sounded more like a threat than a casual closing to a conversation.

I hope his big ego is bruised because I didn't fall all over myself for being offered a chance to roast hot dogs with him, Spring thought vindictively and then sighed. It might have been fun, if his reasons for asking had been the right ones.

She went into the house, and showed off her new clothes to Mrs. K and then went up to her room to put them away. She realized she'd better come up with something plausible to tell Reed she was doing Saturday night. Should she call an old school chum? Mary Louise, maybe? But Mary Louise had seemed strangely withdrawn from Spring before Spring had left for school three years ago. Her answers to Spring's letters had been long in coming, and then stilted and awkward when they did come. Considering that, Spring thought, maybe it would be better if Mary Louise made the first move in renewing old acquaintances. The grapevine would let her know Spring was home.

Réjean, she thought, suddenly remembering the phone number that was crumpled in a careless ball in the bottom of her purse. She fished it out and looked at it, hesitating. Well, why not? she asked herself, annoyed with her hesitation. It was that same kind of hesitation that had always prevented her from accepting many dates at college. She always felt a strong emotion of dishonesty when she agreed to go out with young men. It was too easy to compare them to Reed and find them coming up short.

And yet it was ridiculous not to ever go out, to live like a nun in a cloister, Spring chided herself with her roommate's words. Carolyn had never given up scolding her for spending so many evenings squirrelled away with a book when she had opportunities to be doing other things.

"For God's sake," she'd snap, "it's no crime to go out with a member of the opposite sex. Big boys and girls do it every day, Spring!"

So it was no big deal. He'd asked her to a movie, and she was going to accept. Big boys and girls did it every day. She marched downstairs and into Reed's office before her fragile resolve could disappear. She hesitated again, took a deep breath and picked up the phone.

It rang several times, and Spring found herself hoping Réjean wasn't home. But then he answered, and her nervousness was dispelled slightly by the surprised warmth in his greeting.

"I was just thinking that maybe a movie Saturday would be a nice idea," Spring told him awkwardly.

He was delighted, asked for directions to the orchard and told her he'd be there about eight o'clock.

Perfect, Spring thought, Reed would already be gone.

"I'll see you Saturday then, Spring. I''m looking forward to it."

"I'm looking forward to it, too, Réjean," she replied politely, though she was already wondering if she hadn't made a mistake. She hung up the phone and turned around to find Reed standing her the door behind her, his arms folded across his chest and his face glowering.

"Who the hell is Réjean?" he asked thunderously, crossing to her and thwarting her half-formulated plan to try dashing by him. He towered over her, his face harsh, a muscle flicking impatiently in his jaw.

Spring caught herself shrinking from him and defiantly squared her shoulders. She had nothing to feel guilty about, she reminded herself firmly.

"He's a friend of mine," she answered cautiously.

"Oh? Funny, I don't remember anybody named Réjean from your school days. I usually have a good memory for names."

"He's not from my school days," she conceded, feeling herself to be on very shaky ground, though she wasn't certain why.

"Vancouver, then?" Reed asked silkily. "An old college friend?"

"No. I met him today. At the library." The library seemed to add a measure of respectability, she thought, then reminded herself there was nothing disrespectable about meeting a young man and agreeing to go to the movies with him. "He's taking me out Saturday night."

Reed drew in his breath savagely. "What?"

"We're going to a movie," she informed him, but the steadiness of her tone was fast fading under the raking anger in his eyes.

"Good heavens, woman!" he rasped, pushing the hair off his forehead with leashed violence and shifting his gaze to the window. Her respite didn't last long—a few seconds later his blazing eyes were once again focused on her. "Didn't it mean anything to you?"

"What?" she whispered, but she needn't have because she knew he was referring to the episode in the orchard this morning. "Well, did it mean anything to you?" she snapped, trying to hide her uneasiness. What was he so angry about? He had made a date himself for Saturday night, hadn't he?

She found her shoulders trapped in the painful, biting grip of his hands, and he shook her hard. "What the hell do you think?"

She didn't know what she thought. Her mind was reeling with confusion. She knew what she'd thought after that kiss, but then Penny had come along. Penny had come along and said they were more than friends, and he hadn't disagreed. In fact, he seemed to have been passing out the recipe for winning his heart.

Reed, she said silently, I know what I want to think, but I also know how dangerous it is for me to think it. You're so complicated. One minute boyish and affectionate, and the next hard and cold. How can I risk telling you my heart? Once I thought I knew you; once I told you everything. But I can't trust you anymore. I don't know what motivates you. I don't fully understand the mystery that lurks behind those jade-green eyes.

"It was a pleasant interlude this morning," she managed, amazed at her composure. "I guess I thought it was rather interesting that you'd decided to take responsibility for that particular aspect of my education."

He released her shoulders with such abruptness that she nearly tumbled backward. His hands fell to his sides, and he stared at her, at first with amazement and then with cool distaste.

"To think," he said, his voice chilling, "that I almost believed it. Almost believed the look of innocence—the virginal facade—was real. Oh, you're good, Spring," he said harshly. "I find you in bed with a man one week, and by the next week you have me convinced I must have made some kind of mistake. When I kissed you I was certain. A kiss as sweet and fresh as though you'd never opened those lips to a man before. But any woman who can kiss one man like that in the morning and be rushing off to make a date with another one the same afternoon isn't innocent. Just playing games. And I don't like to be played with, Spring," he said, and the cold warning in his voice made her shiver.

He's turned the tables again, she thought with bitter bewilderment. He's the one playing the games. He's the one telling the lies. He was a part of that kiss, too. Did he conveniently forget that when he was making *his* date for Saturday night? What does he want from me? What on earth does he want from me?

"Well, I don't like to be played with, either," she shouted.

He laughed harshly. "You needn't worry about that ever again." He turned on his heel and left the room, his back stiff with anger.

Chapter Five

Spring made her way cautiously down the wide staircase. The house had been quiet for about fifteen minutes, and she was sure Reed must be gone. It was nearly eight, and Réjean would be here soon. She stopped, listened and sighed with relief. The house was empty. Mrs. K had long since departed for her Saturday-night bridge game, and Judd seemed to live out of doors. Spring smiled. She liked Judd. He was such a nice, uncomplicated man—unlike someone else she knew.

The smile turned to an unconscious frown at the thought of Reed. She'd been going to ridiculous lengths not to find herself alone with him. There was a subtle difference in the tension between them since that kiss and argument. A difference that she couldn't quite pinpoint, yet it both frightened and oddly exhilarated her. She wanted him to kiss her again, but how could she encourage that without proving to him that she was the wanton tease that he'd accused her of being?

At first she'd tried to deny to herself that she wanted to be kissed again. How could she! He was a brute. Unfeeling, harsh and all too prepared to jump to conclusions where she was concerned. And then there was Penny. Spring just didn't feel the confidence to compete for Reed with a woman like Penny. So wanting to be kissed by him made no sense at all.

But these past few days, she'd felt his eyes resting on her with a strange moody light burning in their depths. And she'd felt the strangest sensations in her body.

"Hello."

Spring had wandered into the almost dark living room and was looking out one of the large French windows. With a startled gasp, she turned. "Reed," she stammered, "I thought you'd be gone."

How could she have missed him? He was sitting in a deep leather chair beside the huge old fieldstone fireplace, the white of his shirt almost brilliant in the nearly dark room. Oh God, she thought weakly, he looks devastating. The tailored black pants molded to his long, firm legs, the white of his shirt making him look even more darkly tanned than normal. The shirt, in the style of tux shirts, had ruffles on it. It made him look exceedingly suave and slightly dangerous, like an old riverboat gambler.

"Did you really think I would leave without meeting your beau?" The words were soft and slightly sardonic, reminding Spring he hadn't relinquished his role as her guardian for all else that he might have relinquished.

"Must you treat me as such a child?" she asked softly.

"Perhaps you're mistaking my intentions," he returned blandly.

"What does that mean?" she demanded.

But he didn't answer, his gaze running over her lazily, and she felt that familiar shivering in her stomach.

"Won't Penny be waiting for you?" she asked a little frantically.

"It won't hurt her," he said with a total lack of concern.

Oh yes, Reed, Spring thought bitterly. That's just like you. Never let anybody be too sure of you, never let anybody think there's the slightest chance of taming you. Are you using me, too? As part of your strategy with Penny?

They both heard the engine at the same time, and Reed frowned at the unmistakable sound of a motorcycle but said nothing. A moment later, the doorbell rang.

"Hello, Réjean," Spring greeted her date, but her voice sounded dead in her own ears. "Come in."

"You look lovely," Réjean said, and Spring felt herself prickle at the compliment because it seemed exaggerated. She was wearing jeans and a casual woven top. Now if she'd been in a violet, frothy dress...

She evaluated his appearance through Reed's eyes and felt relief. Réjean looked neat and clean-cut in a light-coloured sports shirt and matching cords.

Réjean looked over her shoulder. "Ah, this must be your uncle."

Reed had come up behind her, and she turned in time to see his eyebrows shoot up.

"I'm Reed Caldwell," he said to Spring's relief, neither confirming nor denying her little white lie. He extended his hand to Réjean, and Réjean introduced himself.

"Would you care for a drink?" Reed asked smoothly, and Spring eyed him suspiciously. She just wanted to get out of here, and she hadn't a doubt that Reed was setting the ground for an inquisition.

Réjean looked pleased. "A beer would be nice, Mr. Caldwell."

Spring sighed resignedly. "I'll get it. Reed, do you want one?"

"No thanks," he said levelly, his refusal putting him and Réjean on unequal footing.

When she came into the living room with Réjean's beer, she noticed that Reed was looking rather intimidating. She hoped Réjean hadn't opened the conversation by telling Reed he was content to live on unemployment insurance for most of the year.

Réjean was looking uncomfortable. "I'll be leaving in a few weeks to start picking the cherries farther south. Probably Penticton."

"Oh? Couldn't you be picking now? Asparagus?"

Réjean wrinkled his nose boyishly, but Spring noted that Reed looked far from charmed. "The asparagus is very hard work, Mr. Caldwell, and very dirty. You lie on a flatbed being pulled by a tractor and eat dirt all day—"

"I'm aware of how asparagus is picked," Reed commented dryly.

"Of course," Réjean said uneasily, staring at his beer. He lifted the bottle to his lips and took a long swig. Reed threw Spring a glance that said his assessment of Réjean was not exactly favorable.

"Shall we go?" Spring asked desperately.

"Yes," Réjean agreed, clambering to his feet eagerly. "It was nice meeting you, Mr. Caldwell."

Reed nodded at him and got to his own feet, picking up his tux jacket. He followed them out the door, watching with his lips in a firm, disapproving line as Réjean strapped the heavy motorcycle helmet onto Spring's head. He got into his car as Spring climbed awkwardly onto the back of the motorcycle.

"The uncle is formidable," Réjean said, and then muttered, *"Bien dans sa peau."*

"What's that mean?" Spring asked curiously.

"It's French, a grudging compliment to your uncle. It translates to something like 'comfortable in his own skin'—very confident. I don't think he liked me, though."

He seemed to want reassurance, but Spring could give him none. The motorcycle roared to life, and she noticed it was only then that Reed started his car.

"I think he intends to follow us," Réjean bemoaned over the roar of the engine. "I'll have to drive like a little grey-haired lady—which is, no doubt, what he wants."

Spring hoped he was wrong. It would be too humiliating. But Reed's car did tail them all the way into Vernon, and she could imagine those stern eyes judging every move Réjean made. She refused to acknowledge Reed's presence with even so much as a glance over her shoulder; and yet, very reluctantly, she had to admit a certain relief that Reed had followed them. Réjean obviously didn't like driving cautiously, and without Reed following like a shadow, Spring had little doubt that she would have been in for a much wilder ride.

The Mercedes left them at Main Street. Réjean found a parking spot close to the theatre and helped her take off her helmet.

"We have a little time before the show. Why don't we stop in at one of the clubs for a drink?"

Spring hesitated. She didn't like to drink, mostly because she'd seen how alcohol transformed her father.

And she didn't much like clubs if the few she'd visited in Vancouver were any indication of what to expect. On the other hand, she felt the evening hadn't gotten off to a very pleasant start for Réjean. Maybe she should make some effort to make amends.

"I guess one drink would be okay."

Réjean smiled at her and took her hand. For a split second, she wanted to jerk it out of his grasp. She really didn't feel like she knew him well enough to be walking down Main Street holding his hand. To her, the gesture held a subtle implication of boyfriend-girlfriend that seemed a bit premature to say the least. Spring grinned to herself. If Reed only know what an old-fashioned prude she really was, he'd probably die laughing. She hadn't dated much—in fact, almost not at all, and she was still preoccupied with questions like whether or not to hold hands and kiss on the first date. The rest of the world, she knew, had moved on. Well, she told herself firmly, it's time to join the rest of the world. She let her hand remain in Réjean's.

The club he took her into was fearfully dark. They stood in the doorway for a moment letting their eyes adjust, and she tried not to cringe from the screamingly loud rock and roll music. It's only for one drink, she reminded herself stoically.

Réjean spotted some friends and pulled her over to them. Loud, enthusiastic greetings in French followed. His hand slipped possessively around her waist while he made the introduction, and once again she had to steel herself not to move away. Though she couldn't understand what was being said to Réjean, she had a niggling suspicion that maybe his friends had been expecting him.

After the introductions a couple of the men made comments to Réjean in French. From their tones and the way their girlfriends poked them, she knew the comments were about her. Spring blushed furiously, trying to tell herself they weren't being intentionally rude.

Réjean signalled a waitress, and when Spring ordered a Coke, he mockingly rolled his eyes. Then he rejoined the conversation with his friends—in French—leaving Spring to feel very much like an outsider. She shifted her attention to the club they were in. It was too dark to pick out any details of the decor, but it actually seemed like a carbon copy of the few clubs she'd been talked into visiting in Vancouver. It had a stand-up bar, tables and chairs, a booth for the disc jockey and a tiny dance area. There was nothing there to hold her attention, so she shifted her gaze to the other customers, feeling a growing sense of unease. She wasn't a snob by any means, but the general dress and deportment of the growing crowd told her that she'd found her way into a rather seedy establishment.

"Réjean," she interrupted him, "I really think maybe we'd better get to the movie."

"Oh," he said easily, "why don't we just skip the show? It wasn't anything I really wanted to see, anyway."

Spring remembered feeling his friends might have been expecting him and looked at him narrowly. Had he ever planned on seeing the show in the first place? She noticed another drink had been placed in front of him, and she wasn't quite sure what to do. She'd look like a shrew if she demanded to be taken to the show. Of course, she could just leave, but she didn't know how she'd get home. She mentally counted the contents of her wallet and realized she didn't even have cab fare.

"I'd like to see the show," she said tentatively. "That's what I told Reed I was doing." And God knows, she added to herself, he's sure to ask for details.

"Come on, Spring," Réjean wheedled, "you're a big girl. Your uncle can't dictate what you're doing every second, even if he is formidable."

That appealed to the rather rebellious side of her, although her logical side was trying to tell her to insist that he either take her to the movie or take her home. She glanced at his face and realized it had a stubborn set to it. Suddenly, she felt trapped.

A round of drinks arrived, and one was placed in front of Spring.

"It's a shooter," Réjean explained to her, evidently dismissing her wishes. "That means you shoot back the whole thing in a single gulp." He demonstrated, and she noticed the others at the table were doing the same, and now they were all watching her with expectant, amused eyes.

"But what is it?" she asked hesitantly.

"It's called a B-52. It's got Kahlua in it, Bailey's Irish Cream and Grand Marnier. Go for it, Spring."

The names meant nothing to her, but she took a tentative sip and smiled politely. "It's very good."

Réjean laughed. "Okay, but sipping is cheating. The whole thing," he encouraged, his eyes merry.

"Oh, I can't. Réjean, I don't drink much, and—"

"Drink," he insisted. "It'll help you relax. You do seem a little tense."

She was on the verge of refusing him and telling him in no uncertain terms exactly why she was tense. But his friends grew impatient, and she discovered that they spoke enough English to begin chanting for her to drink while pounding their fists on the table. To her horror, she found every eye in the place looking toward her with amused interest. She took a deep breath, picked up the glass and swallowed the drink. She blushed to the roots of her hair when the whole bar cheered her.

"Now," she said coldly to Réjean, "I'd like to be taken home before you have too many of these."

He looked at her searchingly and then sighed when he saw that she meant it. "Okay," he conceded, catching her off guard by not arguing. "I'll just finish this drink first."

Relieved to have won the concession, she decided not to push her luck. She nodded her agreement. But then another B-52 was placed in front of her. Wishing not to make herself the centre of attention again, she drank it back like everyone else did with their drinks. Another was placed in front of her, and then another in rather rapid succession.

She glanced at Réjean, woozily suspicious, but it didn't seem to matter very much anymore. Why should she go home to an empty house?

Réjean was so enthusiastically immersed in a loud discussion with his friends that he seemed to have forgotten her completely. So when a fairly clean-cut man came over and asked her shyly to dance, she readily agreed.

She didn't usually care for dancing because it made her feel awkward and self-conscious, but at this moment, she could hardly wait to get on her feet. She danced several dances, amazed by her confidence and ease, and even more amazed that she seemed to be in great demand as a partner. In between dances, she found another drink in her hand. Her present partner smiled at her and told her the drink was a chichi. It was tall, white and frothy, and she found it absolutely scrumptious.

Later Réjean sought her out, looking vaguely unhappy. She laughed at him and teased him for ignoring her. Actually, everything struck her as being rather funny and fun, and she was rather proud of the fact that she seemed unusually witty and outgoing tonight. She and Réjean danced a few dances, but then one of her former partners reclaimed her, handing her a drink she'd forgotten she asked for.

Her newfound popularity astounded her, and she was quite delighted with herself. She was popular! She was the belle of the ball—even if she didn't have a seductive, mauve-tinted dress. The men were paying her outrageous compliments, buying her drinks and practically queuing up to dance with her. If only Reed could see her now!

She had only the haziest idea of time passing, but it did occur to her that it was much later when Réjean caught up with her for another dance, this time a ballad. She noticed with momentary uneasiness that he was holding her far too closely, and that his hand had the oddest way of slipping up to the curve of her breast, even though she kept pushing it down. She didn't want to say anything because she wasn't sure if the caress was intentional or purely accidental.

Besides which, her mind was uncomfortably fuzzy all of a sudden, and it was too much effort to concentrate. Reed, she thought hazily and relaxed against him while imagining green eyes and strong arms around her. There was a loud crashing noise, and Spring opened her eyes to see the bouncers hurl themselves into a fight in one corner of the dance floor. She watched with a strange detachment, feeling safe with Reed—but suddenly she remembered she wasn't with Reed.

I'm drunk, she thought with surprise. In fact, I think I'm very drunk, and I think it's very late. She pulled out of Réjean's tight hold and looked up at him, trying to judge just how much he'd had to drink. A lot, she thought miserably. His eyes had a funny look in them, and his breath smelled sour and unpleasant.

How am I going to get home? she wondered, and suddenly the evening turned as sour as Réjean's breath. The brawl continued, and she noticed a glazed look in people's eyes as they laughed and shouted and made no sense at all. It wasn't fun anymore, in fact it was rather sordid and ugly.

She didn't feel popular or beautiful anymore, either, just like a foolish girl who'd had far too much to drink.

"Réjean, how am I going to get home? You can't drive."

He looked at her with indignation. "Of course I can drive! Well, maybe not all the way out to your place, but I don't live far from here." He smiled at her wickedly. "I want you to come home with me."

Spring stared at him with horrified disbelief, her trapped feeling of earlier returning, only this time even more cloying. She spun on her heel and walked into the ladies' washroom, needing desperately to compose herself so that she could think. She pressed a cold cloth to her head. That first man that had asked her to dance had seemed rather shy and sweet. Was he still sober? Could she trust him to take her home? Maybe she could call the cab company and find out if they'd take her home on credit. She could find some money once she got there. Would Reed be home? She debated whether or not to call him, but he'd be angry and more certain than ever that she was wild and irresponsible. She decided to call Reed only as a last resort. First, she'd call the cab company and see what they had to say. She threw the towel in the bin and walked out in search of a phone.

And then she saw Reed, and the relief swept through her, forcing her to admit to herself how frightened she'd been. He looked incongruous, still dressed in his tux and standing head and shoulders above anyone else in the room. She stood on tiptoe, trying to see over the crowd, who he was talking to. He had Réjean firmly by the arm, and Réjean was gesturing vaguely. Reed squinted through the dark smoke-filled room. He saw her and abruptly dropped Réjean's captive arm, shoving people impatiently out of his way as he walked toward her. A girl stopped him, smiling up at him and hanging onto his arm while she spoke to him. He bent his head, listening for a moment, said something to her and then shook her off when she didn't relinquish her hold.

Then he was in front of Spring, his expression not quite as fierce as she'd expected it might be.

"Are you coming quietly?" he asked over the din, his voice level and calm, "Or is it going to be necessary to drag you out by your ear?" When she opened her mouth to reply, no words came out. He took her firmly by the elbow and propelled her through the crowd. The girl who'd stopped him glared at Spring with open envy and hostility. Spring smiled smugly, wiping the look off her face hastily when Reed glanced down at her.

His car was right outside the door. He unlocked it and shoved her in unceremoniously.

"Don't start on me, Spring," he warned, getting in his own side and starting the engine. "I'm within a hair of turning you over my knee and giving you a walloping you won't forget. Just one word of protest from you—"

"Reed, I've never been so glad to see a person in my entire life," she said quietly, her defenses down, and her speech only slightly slurred.

He shot her a sharp, quizzical look. "Are you drunk?"

"Yes, I'm afraid I am," she murmured sadly.

"Did you have to pick that place? It's got the worst reputation in the valley."

"Does it? Oh, dear, I hope nobody I know saw me, then."

"You don't have to worry about that," Reed said dryly. "Nobody you know would be caught dead anywhere near that place."

"How did you find me, Reed? How did you know I was in trouble?"

"Trouble?" he said, and there was a sudden killing light burning in his eyes. "What kind of trouble? So help me God, if that kid did anything to you, I'll—"

She decided quickly to protect Réjean from that fierce gleam in those clear jade eyes. "Oh, Reed, nothing like that. Only I just figured out that Réjean couldn't drive me home, and I didn't know what I was going to do. I didn't have enough money for a cab, and I didn't know if they'd take me all the way out there on credit. I was so glad to see you, even though I was scared to phone you. Do you suppose I sent you a telepathic message?" she asked him seriously.

He groaned. "You are drunk. No, I didn't receive any telepathic messages. I got home late. You weren't home, and the movies had been out for hours. That left the bars, and the unfortunate probability that after a few hours in a bar you would try to come home on that motorcycle. I went to every bar in town before I tried that one."

"Did you? Are you very angry?"

"Very," he agreed dryly, without elaborating.

"Oh." She studied her hands for a few moments and then shot him a glance from under the silky curtain of her lashes. The last thing she wanted to do was laugh, but she remembered him coming into the bar looking so wonderful and so out of place that she couldn't stop herself. Her own white knight sweeping in to rescue the damsel in distress.

"It's not a laughing matter," he told her sternly.

"I know," she agreed humbly, "but, Reed, you did look so funny coming in there in a tux, and people were gaping at you like you were some kind of celebrity... and it was just funny."

She expected him to bite her head off. Instead she heard a low rumble from him and realized that he was laughing too.

"I guess you're not the only one who thought so. Did you see the rather—er—inebriated young lady who way-laid me?"

Spring nodded.

"She wanted my autograph. She thought I was that television actor—the one who plays a private eye."

Spring looked at him thoughtfully. "You don't look anything like that guy," she decided firmly.

"No?" he said, pretending disappointment.

"Oh, no. You're much nicer looking than him," she told him guilelessly. "Are you done being mad now?"

He looked at her, a reluctant smile tugging on his lips. "Spring, I can never seem to stay mad at you."

"Can't you?" she whispered, trying very hard to be sober.

"No," he said, then turned his attention to the dark highway unfolding in front of him.

She stared at the outline of his face, lit up slightly by the lights on the dash. The playfulness was gone from his features, and his expression was once again stern and unreceptive. Spring sighed, drawing his eyes to her.

"Did you and Penny have a good time tonight?" she asked, hoping that he wouldn't guess the real reason for that heartfelt sigh.

He shrugged. "I don't like Penny's stuffy old benefit balls, but on the other hand, it's pretty hard not to have a good time when you're with Penny."

"Oh," Spring said with pretended indifference, though the remark went like a barbed arrow to her heart.

"I wish you liked her, Spring," he said softly.

"Did she tell you I didn't?" Spring demanded.

He looked startled. "No." His features were once again formidable. "Did *you* tell *her* that you didn't like her?"

"Of course not. But she's very perceptive."

Reed sighed. "So am I, where you're concerned. I knew you didn't like her when I saw you together after you'd been shopping. And like I said, I wish you did."

"Why?" she asked, and then wished she hadn't. She knew why, she thought wearily. It was because Reed loved Penny. Maybe wanted to build a life with her, and he was worried about how they would get along. But she didn't want to hear it from his own lips.

Reed shrugged, his face impassive. "Penny's had a hard life. And she means a lot to all of us—to Mrs. K, Judd and me. She's like a member of the family, and in fact..." His voice drifted off, and he looked thoughtfully at the road. "It would just be better all the way around if you liked her," he finished abruptly.

Spring felt sick. What had he almost said? That soon Penny would be a member of the family? Officially? But what was the holdup then? Penny wanted to marry him, and he wanted to marry her, so what was stopping them?

Me, Spring thought dully. No wonder they're both so eager for me to like her. But I can't. And especially not now I can't.

But there were other puzzles. If Reed loved Penny, why didn't Penny seem to know? Was it just because he played his cards so close to his chest? Reed did make it difficult for people to guess what he was thinking and feeling. The question was a little too much for Spring's booze-befuddled brain, and she was relieved to see that they had turned onto the lane leading to the house.

Her legs seemed to have grown oddly mushy on the journey home. To her embarrassment, Spring had to have Reed help her into the house and up the stairs to her room.

"Get into bed," he commanded gently. "I'll be back in a minute to tuck you in."

She quickly put on her nightie and hopped into bed. "Reed, the room is spinning," she announced when he returned with a glass of water.

He grinned at her and shook his head. "It's all part of the fun," he told her cheerfully. "Try putting one leg on the floor. That might help."

She did as he told her, and the room stopped spinning. "How did you know that?" she asked, relieved.

"Oh, I had a few wild and crazy days in my youth. Mostly when I went to university." He passed her a couple of aspirin and a glass of water. "This is one of the ways I used to try to prevent a well-deserved hangover. I can't remember how well it worked, though."

She took the aspirins and swallowed them with the water. "I'm glad you don't drink very much, Reed. I don't think I like what it does to people."

"It's nice to know you like something about me, Spring," he teased her.

The liquor made her bold, and she smiled at him. "That's not all I like about you, Reed."

"Oh? What else do you like, sugar?"

"You haven't called me sugar for a long time," she said dreamily.

"Haven't I? Tell me what else you like about me."

Her eyes seemed to catch on his lips, and although she tried, she couldn't shift them away. "I liked the way you kissed me, Reed. Would you kiss me?"

"No," he said gently and firmly. "I won't."

"Why not?" she asked, pouting.

"Because you're very drunk. Good night, Spring." He turned and walked away, then paused at the door, looking back at her with strangely unreadable eyes.

"Spring, why did you tell Réjean I was your uncle?"

She twisted her hair uncomfortably in her hands, looking intently at the golden strands. "He asked about my father, and I told him Daddy was dead. I started to tell him I lived with you, but it didn't sound very good. I mean, we are living together but not in the way that people usually are when they say they're living together, and I didn't want him to think—"

"That we were involved? No, he wouldn't have asked you out then, would he?"

"Oh, no, Reed, that's not it at all! I didn't want him to think my living here was dirty or ugly, or lewd. I mean I know it's not, and you know it's not, but...oh, I don't even know what I'm trying to say."

"It's all right, Spring. I know what you're saying."

"Do you?"

He looked at her for a long time, his expression thoughtful. Finally he spoke, his voice as soft as the breeze that was blowing through her window.

"Spring, can you understand how it was for me? When I sent you away?"

She stared at him, and for a painful moment, she could understand. But she didn't want to understand, she realized, because if she understood, then she would have to forgive him. And if she forgave him, she couldn't hate him anymore. And if she didn't hate him anymore, she would have no choice but to love him. But her heart would only be broken again because now there was a whole new set of problems, the biggest one being Penny... the woman that Reed implied he was going to marry.

She was aware that he was still standing in the door watching her, and waiting for her answer, and she steeled herself against the look in his eyes. What was that look? More than sadness, somehow, more than pleading... and she could put him out of his misery. She could say, right now, *Reed, I understand. I understand that it was hard, and I understand you did it for me, and I'm sorry.*

She pushed away her brief understanding. "The situation is not at all the same," she said coolly, feeling suddenly very sober.

He watched her for a moment more, then turned and quietly shut the door behind him. His broad shoulders had been slumped, she noted dejectedly, like those of a weary, defeated man.

What have I done? she asked herself despairingly. *What have I done?*

Chapter Six

Spring wandered into the kitchen rather late the following morning, surprised to find Judd still sitting there nursing a cup of coffee. She had a slight headache, and her mouth tasted awful even though she'd brushed her teeth several times. But physically she felt grand, compared to how she felt emotionally.

"I just can't believe that Reed would take off at this time of year," Mrs. K was saying to Judd. "It's just not like him to go when there's so much work to be done." She turned and frowned thoughtfully at Spring. "Did you have another fight with him?"

"It wasn't exactly a fight," Spring muttered. "Where did Reed go?" And why do I feel so sad that he's gone? she added to herself.

"He didn't say where he was going or how long he was going to be," Judd said. "But his car looked like it was full of camping gear, and he had a look like thunder on his face. I wasn't about to start asking him questions."

Mrs. K sighed breezily. "Well, goodness if he isn't acting like a man in love."

"Well, he is in love," Spring snapped. She wondered dully if Penny was accompanying him on his trip. Had he known about it last night? Or even worse, had she forced him to turn to Penny for solace by being so lacking in understanding?

"You don't seem very happy about it," Mrs. K said, looking at her shrewdly.

"Well, I can't say that I see love being anything to be happy about, either," Judd said, winking widely at Spring. "Especially if it makes a man lose his head like that."

"Judd Black," Mrs. K said sternly, shaking her wooden spoon at him, "You know darn well you don't believe that. And when I look at you lately, I rather doubt that *you* have a head to lose. I've seen that calf-look in your eyes, and it's about time you did something about it."

Judd looked suddenly uncomfortable. "Come on, Mrs. K," he said gruffly. "What have I got to offer a woman? I don't have much money, I'm not the world's smartest person, and God knows, I don't have good looks. A woman would have to be a fool to marry me."

"Oh, Judd," Spring said, staring at him with surprise. "How can you say that? You've got yourself, and I think you're wonderful. You're kind, gentle, sensitive and patient. You're teaching me to drive, aren't you? And you haven't yelled at me once—not even when I hit the tree at the bottom of the driveway. I think a woman would have to be a fool *not* to marry you if you asked her."

Judd was blushing furiously. "Do you really think that?" he asked shyly, toying with his fork, then glancing up at her.

"Of course I do," Spring told him affectionately. "Now, who's the lucky girl?"

"There isn't one," Judd growled, but he was still blushing. He left the table and a moment later he passed under the kitchen window. Spring and Mrs. K could hear him whistling merrily.

"I've been telling him the same thing for years, and he hasn't paid a bit of attention to me," Mrs. K complained. "I suppose he had to hear it from a pretty girl."

"Mrs. K, I'm not pretty," Spring protested.

Mrs. K looked at her sharply. "Oh, love," she said gently, "when did you stop believing you were pretty? As a little girl you never doubted it for a moment. I used to think you were going to grow up quite vain, especially with Reed encouraging you."

It was true, Spring realized with a start. She had always been confident of her attractiveness. It was only after... after that terrible night when she'd proposed to Reed. Somehow she'd always thought that if she'd been beautiful enough he would never have sent her away. Since then, she'd been unable to look in the mirror and find herself pretty. But now, because of last night's fleeting moment of understanding, she realized it had nothing to do with what she looked like.

Intuitively she felt there was even more to his sending her away than Reed protecting her from people's twisted interpretations of their living arrangement. But what? What else was there? Had it something to do with that haunted hurt expression she'd glimpsed so briefly on his handsome face?

"Why do you suppose he went away?" she asked Mrs. K.

"Reed's just a man, Spring, and like most men he doesn't handle his emotions very well—he'd rather pretend that he doesn't have any at all. Men don't like to admit they're ever weak or vulnerable. Reed never shows the world what he's feeling, never has. My guess is he felt his control slipping and decided to get away for a few days rather than let anybody know what he's going through."

"What is he going through?" Spring whispered.

"I guess that's for him to tell you. Not me." Mrs. K smiled softly. "You used to be good for him that way. He wasn't ever afraid to let his emotions show around you. I remember when the call came in about his parents, his face just froze up colder than ice. It scared me—I thought maybe he wasn't feeling anything at all. But then I found the two of you in the barn crying your hearts out, and I wasn't scared anymore."

Automatically Spring's mind turned back the pages to a different night long ago when he'd told her she had to go. His face, she remembered, had been just the way Mrs. K described it—frozen colder than ice, like he wasn't feeling anything at all. Had those frozen features been hiding something? Had she seen a trace of it last night, and had he gone because he knew she'd seen it?

Spring wondered why he wouldn't let her in anymore. Was it because of Penny? Certainly Reed wasn't going to tell Spring how he felt about Penny or about how Spring's coming home might have affected their relationship. Was Penny now the one he turned to? Was she the one he expressed his deepest thoughts to? His fears, his frustrations, his hopes, his dreams?

Spring felt a stabbing pain in her chest at that thought. It hurt worse than anything had ever hurt her in her life. Was he with her now? Was she listening while he told her the girl for whom he'd bought ponies and fixed dolls wouldn't forgive him for doing something he felt he had to do?

"I think I'll go have a coffee with Penny," Mrs. K said, interrupting Spring's train of thought.

"With Penny? Is she here?"

"What do you mean is she here? No, she's not here. She's at her house, or at least that's where she was when I talked to her a while ago."

"You talked to her this morning?" Spring asked, almost laughing out loud with relief. "After Reed left?"

Mrs. K was looking at her like she'd lost her mind, but she didn't care.

"You're the oddest girl sometimes, Spring," Mrs. K commented, but she was smiling all the same.

The Caldwell orchard comprised some fifty acres of apple trees, and there was no way Judd could do all the work himself. But Spring loved working in the orchard, and despite Judd's initial reluctance to accept her help, he soon realized his only alternative would be to hire someone. Her enthusiasm and her knowledge surprised him, and after their first day working as a team, he was completely won over.

Penny Bryer arrived early the next morning looking slightly incongruous in a plaid shirt and a stiffly new pair of jeans.

"I thought I'd come out and offer my assistance," she informed Judd and frowned when he groaned. "One of Spring, and one of me should just about add up to one Reed."

Judd took her hands, studied her long enamelled nails and shook his head. "Penny, you haven't done a day's work outside in your whole life." His eyes drifted to her creamy complexion. "You'll burn to a crisp, not to mention breaking those pretty fingernails."

Penny, however, would not be put off. She whipped a large straw hat and a thick pair of gloves from her bag and regarded Judd stubbornly. "I came to work, and I'm going to work."

Even Spring, who was very suspicious of Penny's motives and was sure it was to win points with the absent Reed, had to laugh at the picture Penny made when she donned her hat and gloves. She looked exactly like a scarecrow—though Spring had to reluctantly admit a quality of natural elegance still managed to shine through.

Judd decided to humour Penny. Neither he nor Spring expected her to last the morning, but Penny surprised them both by working hard, without complaint. And she gave no sign of giving up.

Chalk another one up for Penny, Spring thought moodily when she saw Judd watching her with admiration.

"She's full of surprises, that one," Spring heard Judd mutter to himself.

She most certainly was, Spring thought with some hostility. But darn, it was hard to remain hostile to Penny. The house rang with laughter when she was around. Penny short-sheeted Judd's bed and put salt in the sugar bowl. She was warm and high-spirited, and sometimes Spring couldn't help but respond to that. Despite herself, the bond of shared laughter grew between them. Her vague feeling that she knew Penny from somewhere also grew, but she still couldn't pin it down.

A first she thought the feeling might be traced to a re-
semblance to an actress or a singer, but more recently she
realized it was the mannerisms, the attitude, Penny's way
of looking at things that seemed strangely and pleasantly familiar. Sooner or later, Spring supposed, she'd
figure it out.

But for now, Penny seemed genuinely eager to learn
about the orchard, and she was constantly plying Spring
and Judd with questions. At first Spring debated how
much of her knowledge she wanted to share with Penny,
but Penny's interest and her own enthusiasm for the
subject got the better of her.

"Why apples, Spring? Why not cherries or peaches or
pears?"

"The weather here is perfect for apples," Spring found
herself explaining patiently. "The soft fruits do better
farther south. Here we have cool, crisp nights, and it's
hot during the day." She began to warm to her subject.
"You really have to own your land to make money from
an orchard—that's why Reed does so well. If he was
making mortgage payments it would be a different story.
And you have to know the market. The big market right
now is for Macs—McIntosh—and Reed's doing well because about sixty-five percent of his trees are Mac.
There's also no money in poor fruit, so we concentrate on
quality. We summer-prune to let more light into the trees;
light gives you colour. We use spreaders to control the
way the branches grow. We try to make sure each one gets
maximum light."

"Kind of like Japanese bonsais," Penny exclaimed
with delight.

"Kind of," Spring agreed. "Nobody can afford to be
a dumb farmer. That's why Reed and Judd are always at
seminars on herbicides, spraying and pruning or a dozen

other things that help them to keep up with the technology. Reed's experimenting, too, with new dwarf varieties and grafting.''

Penny looked up at the trees. "For all this hard work, I hope we have a bumper crop this year."

Spring laughed. "You don't want a bumper crop in this business. It weakens your trees. A bumper crop this year means a bad crop next year. That's why thinning and spacing the apples gets so much attention.

"In the fall, of course, picking starts, beginning in September with the Macs and ending in late October with the Red Delicious."

"How do you know when to pick?"

"Size, colour and pressure. Apples store better if they're picked at a certain pressure, determined by a test. I think Reed uses an iodine test."

"Then winter comes, and you can relax," Penny said hopefully.

"Nope. You've been around in the winter, Penny. The trees have to be pruned once they're dormant—when the sap stops flowing. The dead trees are cut away, and Reed overhauls most of the equipment in the winter. The cycle really never stops—as soon as the ground is workable, he'll be out planting new trees." She paused. "Did I mention soil testing and leaf analysis?"

Penny shook her head, and Spring was off....

Spring had hoped that all the physical work would leave her no time for thinking about Reed. But that wasn't the case. Her mind was quite capable of thinking of him exhaustively even when her hands were busy.

Mostly she seesawed about whether or not she should have been more understanding and open to him the night before he left. Could she have forgiven him? One day she would be certain that she should have, but the next she would remind herself blackly that there was more to it than what his motives had been. There was after all, the autocratic way he'd handled sending her away—the fact that he'd made the decision without consulting her, or even investigating all the options and alternatives. And there was still the fact that she felt humiliated that she'd asked this man to marry her, confessed her love, and he'd been totally indifferent. That was pretty hard to forgive!

The object of her mullings and inner arguments walked in a week to the day after he'd left. Penny, Spring, Judd and Mrs. K were all sitting around the kitchen table having dinner and Reed surveyed them from the doorway.

I missed him, Spring thought, trying not to stare at him, but unable to stop herself. His jaw was dark with unshaven beard, giving him a slightly sinister look and making his eyes seem even greener and more glittering. He was dressed in a sports shirt that outlined the powerful muscles in his chest and arms, and a pair of khaki shorts that showed off the lean, long, rippling line of his legs.

It's not the same without him, Spring thought with wonder. Some part of her knew all the time, no matter how busy she was, that he wasn't there. That part of her knew, and it waited. Even though she didn't acknowledge it, she could feel some kind of tension leaving her. The tension of expectation—of waiting for the sound of a certain footfall, the look in a certain pair of eyes, the deep music of a certain voice.

"Am I missing a party?" Reed asked, sitting down beside Penny. He plucked at her sleeve. "Must have been a costume party," he teased. His eyes sought Spring, and despite the playfulness in his voice when he'd addressed

Penny, his eyes looked grim and cold as they rested on Spring.

Penny sniffed with mock indignation. "Costume party, my foot! The survival of your precious orchard rested entirely in my hands for the past week." She grinned. "Well, maybe not entirely; Judd and Spring helped a little bit."

Reed's eyes drifted from Spring's face back to Penny's. He reached for her hand and studied it, running his fingers over the newly developed calluses. "You've ruined your hands," he commented. "There was probably no need for you to help, Penny."

Penny grabbed her hand away from him and scowled. "Spring was working in the orchard, too. I don't see you all worried about her."

"That's different," Reed said, his gaze finding its way to Spring's face again.

Oh sure, Spring thought, dropping her eyes from his, it's different because he doesn't give a damn about my precious hands.

"Why is it different?" Penny demanded.

"Because Spring—" He stopped, obviously changing his mind about what he was going to say. "Grew up here," he finished. The phone rang, and Reed excused himself, going down to his office to answer it.

He came back a moment later and looked at Spring, his expression dark and forbidding. "It's for you," he said tersely.

She answered it, saying nothing after Réjean's warm greeting, only waiting coldly for him to tell her why he'd called.

"I phoned to apologize for the other night. I behaved badly, and I'm sorry."

"Behaved badly?" she practically shouted at him. "You deliberately got me drunk! You told me we were going to a movie, and you never had any intention of going to a movie! You also, as far as I could see, had no intention of taking me home. I think you're easily the most despicable person I've ever met!"

"You're absolutely right," Réjean agreed meekly.

Spring found herself slightly mollified by that.

"Spring, I have no right to ask you for a favor. None at all. But I need your help desperately. You're the only one who can save me."

Spring's common sense told her to tell him to go jump in a lake, but his voice was terribly humble and pleading, and it made her curious about what he wanted.

"What is it?" she asked cautiously.

"My parents are on their way here. If you think your uncle is formidable, you should see my father! And my mother said on the phone last night that she couldn't wait to meet my friends. Dear God, if she meets Jacques, Marie and some of the others..."

"You wouldn't have phoned to apologize if you didn't want something," Spring deduced accusingly.

"That's not true!" Réjean protested, seeming affronted.

"I don't see how I could help you anyway," Spring said.

"Spring, you're such a nice girl. You're just the kind of girl my parents would heartily approve of. They're not going to be here long, and I just thought if you could come out for lunch with us tomorrow—"

"Réjean, I am not going to be a party to your deceiving your parents."

"Spring, please listen to me. My mother is very fragile, very sensitive. She has a bad heart. My older brother died two years ago in a car crash, and I'm all she has left. I'd like her to feel good about me. I don't think it would hurt to leave my mother with her happy illusions that I'm a nice, successful, hardworking boy that she can be proud of."

"If your mother is so sick, and if you're her only living son, why aren't you at home with her?" Spring asked suspiciously.

Réjean sighed. "As I said, my father is formidable. We have enough trouble getting along with all of Canada separating us. If I was looking for a sure way to kill my mother, it would be to attempt to live under the same roof as my father."

"You're exaggerating," Spring informed him primly.

"Not by much. Will you, Spring? Please?"

She hesitated, picturing Réjean's poor old mother, and knowing her sensitivity was being appealed to above her better judgement. But did she really want to be the one responsible for a frail old woman having to let go of her illusions about her son? What would that do to her if she had a heart condition? Spring shuddered.

Réjean sensed her weakening. "There's nobody else I can turn to, Spring. Please."

"Oh, all right," Spring agreed grouchily. "I'll do it, but I won't tell any lies for you, Réjean."

"There'll be no need," he assured her. "Thank you, Spring. You've saved my life."

I thought it was your mother's life we were concerned about, Spring thought wryly. They arranged a time, and she hung up.

Reed was in the living room, and he called her as she tried to slip by him and up the stairs.

"What did he want?" he demanded.

Spring drew in her breath indignantly. "He asked me to go for lunch with him tomorrow."

"Definitely not!"

"I already said yes," she informed him unapologetically, shelving her own doubts about the luncheon.

"What! Well, you can just march right back to that phone and tell him no."

"Reed, I'm twenty-one years old! I will not be dictated to about who I may and may not see. It's humiliating—and unreasonable on your part. You don't understand the circumstances."

"Circumstances?" he hissed. "I know everything I need to know about your dashing Frenchman, Spring, and you're going out with him again over my dead body. Don't you have any pride? He treated you like dirt."

"I don't see how you can stop me, and I wish you'd let me explain—"

"Spring, you are not going, and that is final!"

"History repeats itself," she hurled at him.

"What the hell does that mean?"

"Oh, figure it out for yourself," she suggested testily.

"Are you ever going to let that go, Spring?" he asked quietly.

"No!"

His eyes hardened on her face. "You're not going for lunch with Réjean," he stated with flat authority.

"I am too."

"I said over my dead body, and I meant it. You know better than to cross me, Spring." His voice was soft, dangerously soft.

"You don't frighten me, Reed," she returned, and then scurried from the room because she was indeed a little frightened by the dark and determined expression on his face.

* * *

She didn't call Réjean back, and the next day she was as nervous as a cat waiting for him to arrive. Reed had given no indication that he even remembered last night's conversation, and she wondered if he'd capitulated, as unlikely as that seemed.

Then suddenly he came in the door and stood looking at her with narrow eyes. "You can go to your room," he ordered her quietly.

Spring gasped. "You can't send me up to my room as though I were some wayward eight-year-old," she told him huffily.

His face remained impassive, and his tone was cool. "Right now, Spring."

"You can't make me!"

A gleam appeared in his cold green eyes. "No?" he queried softly.

She realized furiously that he could make her, and she got up from her chair and eyed him angrily. "I hate you."

"That's a fact of which I'm well aware," he said stonily.

She changed tactics. "But I'm going to look like a fool," she wailed.

"Not as much as fool as if you went out with that fast-talking French Casanova again. Are you completely naive?" he queried sharply.

While she still had a shred of dignity, she turned and marched stiffly from the room.

Reed appeared in her doorway a little while later. "You might have told me his parents would be chaperoning this little affair," he said.

"If you recall, you didn't want to hear any explanations," she reminded him haughtily.

"So he talked you into a little plot to impress his parents, is that it?"

"Reed, his mother has a bad heart," she said pleadingly.

"His mother isn't a day over fifty, and she looks like she runs six miles before breakfast."

"His parents are here?"

"It seems they couldn't pass up a chance to see an orchard—especially the orchard Réjean's fiancée lives on."

"Fiancée? Oh, Reed, he promised me he wouldn't involve me in any lies."

"Spring, you seem to collect fiancés like most women collect shoes. What is it about you that makes a man fantasize what it would be like to be married to you?"

"Do they?" she asked with soft surprise.

"Yes, they do," he told her through clenched teeth.

She took a deep breath. "Do you?"

His eyes narrowed, and his lips tightened into an uncompromising line. "Exactly what kind of admission are you trying to goad out of me?" he asked softly, and then shrugged impatiently, dismissing her question. "I'm going to show the Brassards the orchard. I suggest you get dressed for lunch."

"You're going to let me go then?"

"Spring, I don't approve of the deception Réjean is involved in. On the other hand, his parents are charming people." He smiled tightly. "Besides, they very thoughtfully included me in the invitation." He turned and left her.

Reed turned out to be a charming host. He suggested they lunch at the Vernon Lodge, where the dining area was stunningly beautiful. An indoor garden had been cleverly set up, complete with towering palm and rubber trees and other plants. A real creek gurgled merrily through the centre of it. Behind a shield of more palms and towering trees was the hotel swimming pool.

Réjean's parents were a handsome, youthful couple, and at their insistence, Reed told them a little of Vernon's history. It was a subject he was well versed in since his family had played important roles in Vernon's history, helping to pioneer fruit growing in the area.

Though none of the information was new to Spring, she enjoyed hearing it again. In fact, she had to admit that she enjoyed Reed's company in these circumstances. He slipped easily into the role of host, his conversation witty, interesting and knowledgeable. Spring felt proud of him and happy to be at his side. This is what it would be like to be his wife, she mused, and then drew herself up sharply.

Conversation turned to other things, and Mrs. Brassard gave her attention to Spring. "Now tell me, dear, about your plans for the wedding."

"The wedding?" Spring echoed, for a panicky moment wondering if her mind had been read. Then she remembered her supposed role as Réjean's fiancée, and she looked accusingly at him. He pretended interest in his lunch.

You got me into this, she wanted to shout at him, *at least you could get me out.*

But it was not Réjean who came to her rescue. It was Reed. "There isn't going to be a wedding, Madame Brassard," he said quietly and calmly. "Spring had never heard of it before today, and she's occasionally too kindhearted for her own good."

Réjean nearly choked on his steak. His mother was looking at him expectantly, but without too much surprise. He gulped and glared at Reed. "What are you talking about, Mr. Caldwell?"

"The charade has gone as far as I intend to let it go, Réjean. I like your parents, and I respect them, and I think it's only fair that you come clean."

"You accuse me of charades, Mr. Caldwell?" Réjean spat out, his eyes glittering with malice. "What of the charade that you play out? It's fairly common knowledge that Spring isn't your niece. Exactly what is she, hmm? I can hazard a guess, of course. I have eyes. I see the way you look at each other, with a kind of hunger that can't mean much except—"

Spring was so furious that the room seemed to be turning a hazy red in front of her eyes. She had never hated anyone like she hated Réjean. She reached out, almost out of instinct, the palm of her hand on a crash course with his face.

Reed snared her wrist easily and drew her hand underneath the table, where he held it firmly.

"Spring is not my niece," Reed said calmly. "As you said, that's fairly common knowledge. She told you that, I think, because she didn't want our relationship left wide open to speculation—like you're doing right now. Spring's father was my orchard foreman. When he died, I became Spring's guardian."

Mrs. Brassard was staring at Réjean with unconcealed horror, and now she found her voice. "Mr. Caldwell, there is no need for you to make explanations to us. I apologize for my son for the embarrassment he's caused you and for the lies he's told." She looked at Réjean sadly. "I thought you had changed. I really thought maybe you had grown up."

Mr. Brassard could contain himself no longer, and he let fly with a long harangue, the meaning of which could not be mistaken even though he'd spoken in his own tongue. Réjean listened and then got up and stalked from the table.

"His father just told him that he will have to come home," Mrs. Brassard explained with an apologetic smile. "He's a difficult boy, the youngest of eight brothers and sisters. I'm afraid he's been spoiled by all of them, including his father and me. His father wants him to come home and work for his brother, where we can keep an eye on him. His brother is a contractor; Réjean doesn't much care for hard work, but in the end he'll come. I hope you'll forgive us, Mr. Caldwell. This didn't turn into a very pleasant outing for you."

"Or for you, I'm afraid," Reed returned easily.

"As for you, young lady," Mrs. Brassard began, leaning forward and lowering her voice to a barely audible whisper, "I knew Réjean was up to his old tricks when he introduced you as his fiancée. It wasn't possible. You see, he was right about one thing—what you feel for Mr. Caldwell is hidden, yes, but there is still something there. Réjean felt it, and I feel it." She smiled. "And set your heart at ease, little one, this 'something' is not just radiating from you."

Chapter Seven

Spring threw another pebble in the creek. French people, she decided grouchily, are just incurable romantics, that's all. The lunch with Réjean's parents had been a week ago, and ever since then Spring had been studying Reed closely to see if he radiated "something." He didn't. If anything, he was cooler and more unapproachable than ever.

She had also been evaluating her own reactions to Reed, trying to determine if there was indeed "something" in them that could lead to the kind of conclusions Rajean and his mother had reached. She was quite relieved to find, in her own mind anyway, that there wasn't. She managed to treat Reed with the same coolness and indifference that he showed her.

Still, if she were going to be absolutely honest, she had to admit that she was feeling something that she couldn't quite put her finger on. A strange quickening of her heart whenever he was around and an even stranger longing when he was not. She was still subjected to those intense physical sensations when she thought about that lingering kiss in the orchard. She admitted what she felt for Reed now was far different than what she'd felt for him as a child, but she was also determined that it wouldn't radiate from her. And she always cut her musings short before arriving at the point where she had to define what that "something" might be.

"Spring."

"I'm by the creek," she called, shivering a little as she recognized the voice.

She heard Reed coming up behind her but she didn't turn. Out of the corner of her eye, she saw him sit down on the grassy bank beside her.

"Who are you daydreaming about now?" he asked, his voice only faintly teasing—something harsher riding only slightly below the surface.

"No one," she snapped, and then sighed. Did they always have to start on this angry note? "It's just beautiful down here," she explained, trying to diffuse the hostility that had leapt up between them.

Reed's eyes followed her gaze to the merrily gurgling creek, to the fronds of the weeping willow that swept down until they touched the dancing surface of the water. His face softened slightly. "Can you feel them weeping?"

Spring lifted her face to the fine spray of mist that came down from the trees. "Yes," she said softly. There was something romantic about the weeping of the trees, she thought to herself, as if they collected the tears of broken loves. She laughed shakily, and inwardly chided herself for being part French.

She was very aware of Reed sitting beside her, of his arms wrapped around his knees, of his fresh, invigorating scent and of the brooding look chiselled into the firm lines of his face. She closed her eyes. If only he would reach out ... touch me ... kiss me ...

Reed stood up abruptly, giving her the uneasy sensation that he had read her mind and found her thoughts unpalatable.

"Mrs. K wondered if you would go into town and pick up a few things for her." He smiled, but the smile did nothing to dispel the brooding look that darkened his eyes. "She's certainly enjoying the fact that you got your license."

"Of course I'll go."

Reed dug into his pocket and produced a list and a set of keys. He passed them to her.

Spring stared at the keys. "Maude?" she whispered, looking at him with surprise. "Reed, I've only had my license for a few days. Are you sure?"

"I trust you, Spring." He paused, then added softly, "What's mine is yours."

She continued to stare at him, trying to discern just what he meant. Was he saying he'd decided to trust her in all things, or was this conversation really just about a car? And what could he possibly mean by "what's mine is yours"? His face was blank, and his eyes faintly hooded, offering her no clues and no answers.

He bent suddenly, kissed her on the tip of the nose and strode away.

She barely noticed the drive into town, and barely appreciated the feel of the powerful car that was in her control. Reed had to be the hardest man on earth to understand.

Since he'd come back from his trip, he'd been aloof and distant almost beyond belief. He barely spoke to her, never smiled at her, and when she caught him looking at

her, his eyes always held that brooding, thoughtful light.
A light she interpreted as meaning now that he had her
home, he wasn't quite certain what to do with her. But
once, she remembered, she'd been out by the creek in the
black shorts and white top that Penny had insisted she
buy,

It had been hot that day, exhaustingly, drainingly hot.
Spring had fallen asleep under the cooling mist of the
willows. She'd awoken feeling that she was being
watched. She turned and saw Reed leaning against a
nearby tree and looking at her. The expression on his
face, she recalled, had quickly become guarded, but for
a fleeting moment she'd glimpsed a light burning in his
eyes that had made her heart begin to hammer thunderously against her chest. Intellectually, she had no idea
what the searing heat in his eyes could have meant, but
emotionally...

Without a word, Reed had turned and disappeared into
the orchard, leaving her feeling strangely tense and un-
fulfilled.

And now today, he told her he trusted her. But did that
mean he was willing to admit he'd been wrong about her
relationship with Rob? He'd kissed her on the tip of her
nose, as if he'd come to the conclusion that she was an
innocent child, yet Spring had to admit that she far pre-
ferred the mysterious light in his eyes the day he'd
watched her sleeping.

"I trust you," he'd said. "What's mine is yours." It
had been spoken with such soft intimacy, almost like a
vow. Almost like a wedding vow, she thought with a
start, and then blushed at her own dreaminess. She forced
her mind away from that strangely enticing thought,
knowing her imagination could easily build it into something that wasn't there at all.

She entered Vernon, closing the subject in her mind, and remembering that she'd been entrusted with a very expensive car. She parked Maude carefully downtown, pushed Reed from her mind and consulted Mrs. K's list.

An hour later Spring double-checked the list and sighed with relief. She had everything. The midday heat had left her cotton shirt sticking to her, and she impulsively ducked into a coffee shop to get a lemonade before driving home. Sissy, she teased herself, knowing the temperature had reached only about eighty-five.

Spring had just turned from the counter when she spotted the familiar face.

"Mary Louise!" she squealed. Mary Louise looked up, and though her face lit up with a smile, Spring was sure she noticed the faintest trace of reserve. Spring's enthusiasm waned a bit as she studied her friend. What on earth was wrong with Mary Louise?

"Can I join you?" Spring asked a little uncertainly. She found some comfort in the fact that Mary Louise's physical appearance was virtually unchanged. She was a classic carrot-top with huge blue eyes, her thin face still covered with the much-despised freckles of her youth.

"Of course," Mary Louise said, but again Spring thought her friendliness seemed slightly strained. "I heard you were back, and I've been meaning to call, but . . ." She picked up her coffee cup nervously.

A diamond glinted on her engagement finger, and despite Mary Louise's odd attitude, Spring couldn't prevent another squeal. She took Mary Louise's hand and examined the ring. "It's lovely. I'm so excited for you! Who are you marrying? Is it somebody I know?"

"Jimmy Allen," Mary Louise said in a voice soft and husky with wonder.

"Jimmy Allen? That's wonderful! Oh, Mary Louise, you've loved him forever. It's just like a fairy tale. I'm so happy for you."

To her amazement, Mary Louise's bottom lip began to tremble, and she looked away quickly to hide the glint of tears in her eyes. "Darn it, Spring," she said shakily, wiping hastily at her eyes, "stop being so nice to me."

Baffled, Spring stared at her. "What on earth are you talking about? We've been best friends since the first day of school."

"Some best friend I turned out to be," Mary Louise mumbled, then looked at Spring with large watery eyes. "Was it awful? Was it just awful at that stuffy old school?"

Spring thought back to her brief days of private school. For as much as she resented Reed for sending her there, she couldn't bring herself to say the experience was awful. In fact, she was a little startled that she resented St. Lucias being called stuffy. It hadn't been stuffy at all! Goodness, there'd been panty raids, soccer games and chattering with friends long into the night. There had been the rapid maturing of flighty, young girls into women as school days drew to a close. Spring was stunned to realize that she cherished her experiences there. She'd learned about art, music and literature. And that newfound appreciation had been able to fill some of the social gaps at college. Spring even owed her friendship with her old roommate, Carolyn, to St. Lucias.

She began to realize that Reed hadn't made an entirely rotten decision, and she swiftly turned her attention back to Mary Louise.

"It wasn't so bad," Spring told her friend, puzzled by the painful look in those china-blue eyes. "Tell me what's wrong," she encouraged gently.

"Don't you know? Didn't Reed ever tell you?"

"Didn't Reed ever tell me what?"

"I thought he would've told you. That's why I had so much trouble writing. That's why I didn't phone you. I thought you'd hate me, and maybe you should because that's not even the worst of it."

"Mary Louise, I haven't a clue to what you're talking about. Slow down and start at the beginning."

Mary Louise drew in a deep, shuddering breath. "Spring, after your dad died, Reed came to see my parents. He asked them if you could come and stay with us until you finished school. We were the natural choice— you and I being best friends, and Mom and Dad having that huge house with six spare bedrooms..." Her voice faded away, and she stared at her coffee. "They said no, Spring. Oh, you know them. They're such atrocious snobs. Dad called your father the town drunk. He said that he certainly never encouraged me to be so friendly with someone so far below my station and that he was drawing the line at having you move in with us. Do you believe that?"

Spring believed it. Mr. Horner was one of the worst stuffed shirts she'd ever met. And she'd always suspected he looked for the sins of her father in her. Spring had simply never cared, she understood with a start, because Reed had instilled in her a sense of her own self-worth that transcended the opinions of the Horners of the world.

"I thought Reed was going to kill him," Mary Louise continued, her eyes wide with remembrance. "I've never seen a man look so dangerous in my life. But he didn't even raise his voice. Just thanked Mom and Dad for their time and left."

"Mary Louise," Spring chastised her gently, "surely you're not taking responsibility for a decision that had nothing to do with you? It was your parents that said no, not you. How could you think that I would hold that against you? I know you would have said yes had the choice been yours."

"But that's just it," Mary Louise wailed. "I wouldn't have."

"What?" Spring stared at her friend without comprehension.

"Oh, Spring, he asked all over the place. He asked Sara's folks, and they really wanted to, but they still had five kids of their own at home sharing three bedrooms. And he asked Leanne's parents. They said yes, but then somebody told him Leanne's dad hit her mom every now and then, and he wouldn't let you stay there. And every time I heard he'd tried something else and failed I was glad! Do you understand me, Spring? I was glad you were going away! That's what a wonderful person I am! That's what a fine best friend I turned out to be."

Spring looked at Mary Louise, too shocked to know what to say. Her friend was crying again and blowing her nose loudly. "But why?" Spring finally asked her softly.

"Because I loved him!" Mary Louise sobbed.

"Reed?" Spring asked incredulously.

"No, of course not. I mean I did have a childish crush on Reed once. We all did. Jimmy Allen. I loved Jimmy Allen."

"But I don't see what that has to do with me," Spring said with confusion.

Mary Louise searched Spring's face suspiciously, then sighed. "You were probably so starry-eyed over Reed that you didn't even notice."

Spring flushed. "Notice?" she prodded.

"Jimmy Allen's been trailing you around like a love-sick puppy since we started school. Don't you remember, Spring? He was always pulling your hair, trying to steal kisses and asking you to dance. He never noticed anybody else. Then when he turned nineteen and got his car, he was always up at your place, pretending to be borrowing stuff or pretending he wanted Reed's advice. And then there was me—skinny, buck-toothed Mary Louise in the background. Why would he even look at me as long as you were around? And you didn't care about him. You didn't even know he was alive. It made me just hate you sometimes, Spring O'Hara! And it made me feel guilty that sometimes I hated you. But the guiltiest I ever felt was when I knew you were going away, and I was glad. And I still feel guilty about it."

Spring studied her friend thoughtfully and then smiled warmly. "Mary Louise, don't feel guilty, for heaven's sake. I know just what it feels like to think you're plain and ordinary next to someone else. And it doesn't matter a darn how nice they are, you still dislike them intensely. I would have felt the same way if I thought Reed felt about you the way you think Jimmy felt about me." She stopped suddenly, realizing what she'd said and hoping that Mary Louise hadn't paid attention.

But Mary Louise had. "Spring," she said softly. "Do you still love Reed?"

Well, Spring thought, there it was. The million-dollar question. The question she never asked herself, the question that she avoided in a thousand different ways, the question that lurked always in the back of her mind, waiting for her to acknowledge its presence. Do you still love Reed? After all the charades and pretenses, after all the denials, after all the arguments and misunderstandings, the question was still there. Now, unexpectedly, it was out in the open, and Spring found she didn't have the strength to deny or fight it anymore.

"Yes," she said wearily. "I still love Reed."

"And?" Mary Louise asked eagerly.

Spring looked at her sadly, feeling a thousand years older than her. "There is no 'and,'" she said softly and firmly.

"But Spring—"

Spring got up abruptly. "I think I'm running late, and Mrs. K will be wondering what happened to me. I'll have to dash. But I'm glad I ran into you, and I'm glad that you told me. And now that you don't have to worry about Jimmy trying to steal kisses from me, I hope we can be friends again."

Mary Louise toyed with the gold chain on her wrist. "Spring, I want to be, but I'm still a little afraid of you— of how Jimmy's going to react to seeing you again."

Again Spring felt aeons older than her friend. "Mary Louise, if you're going to marry him, you'd better make certain that you can trust him. A marriage can work without a lot of ingredients, but not without that one."

Reed trusts me, she remembered and felt a little shiver of pure joy run through her. *And I trust him,* she admitted slowly, almost painfully—especially after what Mary Louise just told her. But then she realized that Mary Louise's revelations had nothing to do with her trusting Reed. That no matter what she'd said and done, in some secret part of herself, she'd never really stopped trusting or loving Reed. She'd only told herself that to lessen the pain of his not returning her love.

"Spring," Mary Louise said, drawing her attention abruptly from her thoughts. "I know you're right, and even though it scares me, I think it's time I faced it. Jimmy and I are having a barbecue at his orchard on

Friday night. Would you come? All of you—Reed, Judd
and Mrs. K?'' She smiled wryly, ''And I guess if the rest
of you are coming, I might as well expect Penny.''

Penny, Spring thought sourly. ''Of course we'll come,''
she responded absently, but she was aware that her joy of
seconds earlier was gone. She'd forgotten about Penny,
but Mary Louise's casual inclusion of her in the invitation made it quite clear that everybody in the valley must
be aware of Penny's close association with Reed. So what
did trust between herself and Reed matter? They weren't
ever going to be building a life together.

She said goodbye to Mary Louise, again promised to
see her Friday and walked wearily out to the car.

What was she going to do? she thought. She couldn't
stay. Not now, not now that she admitted that she loved
him and that she had never stopped. She couldn't stay to
see him marry Penny, to watch their children born.

Funny, she thought dully, I never thought about him
married—not to someone else. It never even occurred to
me when I was in school that Reed might meet somebody and fall in love. I wonder why I never thought of
that? And I never thought of him with children—no,
maybe I have. But not with Penny's children.

Now that she was thinking of it, she could hardly hold
back the urge to cry. And suddenly and sadly, she knew
she wasn't going to go away—not yet. She was going to
stay and cherish each moment that Reed gave to her.

When the time came, when he married Penny, she
would go. And for the first time, she was aware of the
tremendous responsibility that was part of loving another person. She knew she could never tell him why she
was leaving because it would only hurt him, it would only
cause him to suffer.

She felt something close to self-hatred for all the suffering she'd caused him already. If she loved him, she told herself, she should be prepared to love him without a price tag—and demanding to be loved back was a price tag.

If she loved him enough, she should be willing to let him go. His happiness lay in other directions—even if that other direction was another woman's arms. Wasn't that really love? Wanting the very best for your beloved without having your own selfish interests and desires at heart? Wanting his happiness and his contentment above all else?

When she got out of the car later, Spring was unaware that there had been the subtlest of changes in her. Her eyes had a brave and soft light glowing deep within their black depths. It was the look of a woman who fully and deeply understood the ways of love and who courageously accepted all the lessons it had to teach her. It was not a joyous look, but it wasn't entirely painful. Spring's eyes held mystery—the intriguing mystery of all that it is to be a woman.

Despite her resolve, her courage faltered that evening when she approached Reed. She had gone over what she wanted to say, and yet even now, looking at him, she could feel the words catching in her throat.

"Do you want to go for a walk?" she blurted out.

He looked surprised. "Sure."

They walked for a long time in silence, and then Reed reached out and slipped her hand into the cup of his. Suddenly she didn't feel uncomfortable or shy anymore. Her hand seemed to have been made to fit together with his, and she reminded herself of her promise to enjoy each moment that he gave her.

"What's on your mind, sugar?" His voice was deep and gentle, and touched her like a caress. Without looking up into his eyes, she knew he would be watching her, and she knew his eyes would hold tenderness and not that harsh unreadable light that was in them so often these days.

She took a deep breath. "I want to tell you the truth about Rob," she said and felt him stiffen. She was relieved that he didn't let go of her hand.

Slowly she told him the whole story—even about Cap's Café. When she was finished she studied the ground, half expecting a derisive, disbelieving laugh.

Instead Reed took her chin and tilted her head so that she saw his searching gaze.

"Why didn't you tell me that in the first place?" he asked her softly.

Spring tried to pull away, but he held her chin firmly, forcing her to look at him. "I don't even know for sure, Reed. Except that you were being so high-handed and unfair, and it made me so angry that you would believe that of me, even if the evidence was stacked up against me. And I guess, if I'm going to be really honest, I wanted you to think I was as popular as you thought I was, that men really liked me, and that I had some kind of power over them. But I don't, Reed. I've only been on five dates in my whole life, and none of them ever phoned back." She sighed heavily. "Carolyn used to tease me about being too prim and proper. Actually, she said I was probably frigid."

Reed seemed to sense how that judgement disturbed her, and he pulled her tight against his chest, stroking her hair reassuringly.

"You're not frigid, little one," he murmured into her hair. His lips sought the delicate curve of her neck, and he planted tiny kisses there that made her senses begin to tingle and sing. When his mouth found hers she was ready, and she knew she wasn't frigid. In fact, the passion seemed to erupt in her, hot and searing, as her lips explored the contours of his with insatiable and almost frantic hunger.

He raised his lips from hers, his eyes resting on her face. "Spring, I'm sorry. I should have known. Oh, hell, I did know but..." His voice trailed away, and his eyes moved to her slightly parted lips. With a savage groan he reclaimed them. Spring melted willingly into him, her lips offering him everything that she was.

"Forgive me?" he murmured huskily into her hair, a few moments later.

The husky question reminded her that she had only half completed the task that she had set out to do.

"Reed, I don't have anything to forgive you for. It's you who should be forgiving me. I let you believe those things by telling you half-truths and out-and-out lies, and then I was mad when you believed them." She chuckled softly. "It doesn't make much sense, does it?"

She took a deep breath. "There's something else I want to tell you. Reed, I've been acting like you were the villain in a third-rate movie because you sent me away. I never let on that I liked St. Lucias or that I enjoyed college. I guess I wanted to—to kind of punish you for sending me there. I thought for the longest time that you did it to be mean and to hurt me, and I guess now I know there was more to it than what I was willing to see."

"What brought all this on?" Reed asked, smiling slightly at her.

"I think I started to understand the night that you asked me why I had told Réjean that you were my uncle. But I wasn't ready to admit yet that maybe what you did was best. And I still thought that you hadn't even tried to keep me here. But I saw Mary Louise today, and she told me—"

The smile faded with savage swiftness from Reed's lips, and he let her go abruptly. "I see," he said coldly. "Mary Louise was able to convince you I wasn't a third-rate movie villain. But if she hadn't said anything you still would have thought I was. That's very flattering, Spring."

"Reed—" she began pleadingly.

"Didn't you know—without Mary Louise's kind intervention—didn't you know that I would do everything in my power to keep you here, to make you happy? Didn't you know that I would never intentionally hurt you?"

Spring felt her own anger beginning to rise. Oh sure, she had to tell him the truth about Rob because he didn't have enough faith in her to reach that conclusion himself. Yet when the tables were turned, he had the nerve to expect her to have unquestioning faith in his motives?

"As I recall, you didn't quite do everything in your power," she shot back. "And if you didn't mean to intentionally hurt me that night, I'd hate to see what you could do with intent."

For a moment, a look of complete puzzlement broke in on his anger, and then he paled. "You're quite right, Spring," he said quietly and coldly, "there was one other alternative." He looked like he was going to say something else and then changed his mind. Instead he thrust his hands deep in his pockets, turned and walked away.

Spring stood staring after him, unable to believe what had just transpired. She had wanted to clear the air. She'd had every good intention, and it still turned out like this.

What on earth is the matter with me? she asked herself accusingly. This afternoon I had convinced myself that I could be happy with whatever Reed offered me. I was going to accept it and release him by forgiving him for sending me away. I should have known that in some stubborn, mean part of myself, there's one thing I was holding out—one thing I'll never be able to completely forgive Reed for. It was a test, and I failed.

"You see, Reed," she whispered, "I can't forgive you for not loving me enough to say yes all those years ago."

Chapter Eight

Spring tied the shoulder bands on the sky-blue sundress into careless bows. If I had any guts, she derided herself, I'd be gone by now, and not torturing myself by attending this barbecue—the highlight of which promised to be Penny and Reed.

Then, for at least the hundredth time, she asked herself why he'd kissed her. She reminded herself impatiently that she had already answered that one. He'd kissed her because she'd practically begged him to kiss her by dredging up the fact Carolyn had concluded she was frigid. But Spring had to admit she'd dismissed that judgement when Reed had kissed her the first time in the orchard.

She had no doubt that Reed cared about her, but he cared in completely the wrong way. She was still "little one" to him, and he was still anxious to be there as her advisor and helper through all life's little woes and heartbreaks. If that meant reassuring her that she wasn't frigid, he wouldn't hesitate for a second. She scowled. If he could, he'd probably still be bandaging the scrapes on her knees and the cuts on her fingers....

But there was a small stubborn voice inside of her that refused to be overridden by all her attempts to be reasonable. *Does a man kiss a child like that?* it insisted softly.

"How would I know?" Spring answered it grouchily. "I'm not exactly Miss World Experience when it comes to being kissed."

Oh, you know.... the little voice responded cheerily. Actually, she thought, regarding her appearance, a part of her did seem to know something that the rest of her wasn't acknowledging. Outwardly she'd given up to Penny, yet there was something in her that refused to relinquish Reed. And that something had motivated the dress.

The dress was casual, to fit in with the atmosphere of the barbecue. Despite its simple style, however, it looked rather wonderous on her. The colour was a clear, true pastel, almost startling in its accurate reflection of a summer sky. With her colouring, the effect was quite dramatic—the light colour enhanced the gold of her hair and skin and brought out a stunning intensity in the blackness of her eyes. The bodice hugged her gently curving bosom, and then the dress flared out, sensuously outlining her every movement in swirling fabric.

"I didn't buy it just to get Reed's attention," she excused herself halfheartedly. "After all, there are going to be all kinds of people there that I haven't seen for ages, and," she admitted grudgingly, "mostly I don't want to look like a washed out dishcloth next to Penny."

Penny. There it was again, and she'd come the full circle. If I had any guts, she repeated to herself, I'd be gone by now.

She sighed. She didn't have any guts. Once she'd gotten as far as looking up the number of the bus depot—the day after that last kiss in the orchard, in fact. Well, actually she hadn't quite found the number, she'd just found the phone book and stared at it.

Before she'd opened the cover, she'd heard Reed's voice drifting up from the orchard. She hadn't been able to make out what he was saying, but the sound of his voice, deep and self-assured, had been enough. It had been enough to make her close her eyes and imagine the way he looked when he laughed, the way he looked before his head had dropped over hers and his lips had claimed her lips. She'd put the phone book away without opening the cover.

It was enough to wake up in the morning, hear the shower running and think the strangest thoughts about what he looked like standing beneath it—of his hair curling darkly on his head, the water cascading over his broad back, catching in the tangled hair of his chest like small diamonds.

It was enough to pass him in the hallway and feel their arms brush, enough to sit across from him at the table and drink in the jade of his eyes, the sensuous line of his mouth, the shadow that began to darken on his chin and cheeks around suppertime....

She was imprinting pictures of him in her mind. No detail would be left out so that on the lonely nights that stretched ahead of her, she could close her eyes and turn to the album in her mind, where the pictures would be so real, it would almost be like having him with her. There would be the faint scent of sandalwood, the way he cocked his head slightly when he was listening and the way the muscle in his arms leapt and danced under the taut surface of teak-coloured skin. There would be his eyes—in laughter, sadness and anger, the changing of the green's colour and depth like those many hues that emerged from the mysterious depths of Kalamalka Lake.

"Spring! You're making everybody late," Mrs. K called up the stairs. "And Mary Louise just called to remind you to bring your guitar."

Spring checked her reflection once more, and for a moment she was startled by what she saw. "Why, I'm quite beautiful," she remarked to herself, the statement entirely without conceit and more one of amazed discovery.

It would be enough, she thought, if he looked at me, and I knew he thought so, too.

"Spring!" Mrs. K called again.

"Coming." She pulled her guitar out from under the bed, and taking one more slightly awed look in the mirror, she hurried downstairs.

She came into the living room, at first feeling slightly flustered because Reed, Judd, Penny and Mrs. K were all gathered around waiting patiently for her. And then she remembered the picture she wanted and turned swiftly to Reed to catch his look before it was gone....

Her heart stopped. His eyes darkened, and his lips curved into a faint, unconscious smile. He took a half step toward her, and for a heady moment she was sure he was going to sweep her into his arms. He stopped, but nothing could take the smokey look of appreciation in his eyes from her.

"You look lovely," he said, his voice a low growl, which hid something, yet nothing at all.

Then she noticed Penny standing right beside him at the old fireplace, and her moment was gone.

"You do look lovely," Penny said warmly, casting a thoughtful look at Reed and smiling a funny, secret little half smile.

"Goodness, Spring," Mrs. K said, "You look all grown-up." And then she shot Reed a look that was oddly not very different from the one that Penny had given him.

Spring expected Judd to say something because he was always so nice and such a perfect gentleman, but Judd was looking out the window, a preoccupied frown settled over his homely, kind features.

"I'm going to ride with Reed," Penny announced, looping her arm possessively through his. She leaned forward and winked at Spring. "All part of plan B," she murmured.

Spring noticed for the first time how glamourous Penny looked in a very vogue, green wraparound creation. It looked as if it must have been shipped straight from Paris. The colour even matched his eyes, she thought dully. *Is she picking her clothes now to match his eyes?*

Feeling a little like she'd been relegated to the kiddies' table at a Christmas dinner, Spring trailed Judd and Mrs. K out the door, allowing herself to sneak one wistful look at Reed helping Penny into the Mercedes.

Spring had been to Jimmy Allen's place many times as a child, and she remembered it well. Jimmy had made few changes since his parents had retired and moved into town.

The yard was nearly a full acre, done artfully in decorative trees, shrubs and flower beds. In the centre of the yard was a large swimming pool that had been designed

to look like a natural pond. Its decks were made out of
large slabs of flat, dark stone with the rough edges facing outward, forming a wall that provided privacy. Off
to one side was a large patio of the same stone with a
permanent fieldstone barbecue at one end of it. Farther
back, she knew, was a bonfire pit, set in a grove of trees.

"Spring!" Jimmy Allen was upon her. Without hesitating, he picked her up and whirled around with her as
though she were a favorite kid sister come home. She
looked at him cautiously, remembering Mary Louise's
fears, but she saw only puppyish delight in his greeting.
She returned his smile without reserve.

"You're looking great," he exclaimed boyishly.

Spring laughed. "So are you. And the yard is looking
as wonderful as ever."

Mary Louise had come up beside him, scanning his
face fearfully. But then she smiled, evidently seeing only
what Spring had seen. Jimmy wrapped a long freckled
arm around Mary Louise's tiny waist and smiled down at
her. "Kiss me goodbye, sweetheart. Spring and I are
eloping." His tone was gently teasing, letting Mary
Louise know her fears had not gone unnoticed—and that
they were completely unfounded.

"Light the barbecue first, would you?" Mary Louise
returned lightly, but her eyes on his face were serious and
spoke clearly. They said thank-you.

She turned to Spring. "As for the yard, I don't want to
brag, but I did it all. This idiot—" she punched Jimmy
lightly on the arm "—was going to mow it all under after his parents retired, so that he wouldn't have to look
after it."

"That's why I'm marrying her," Jimmy told Spring in
a stage whisper. "Needed a gardener. Not to mention a
cook."

The banter continued between them, and Spring felt herself being drawn into the circle of their affection. *If only,* she thought, *Reed and I could*— But she cut herself off short. She was here to visit with some old friends—maybe, she reminded herself dramatically, for the last time. She wasn't going to allow herself to spoil this evening with self-pity and musings over might-have-beens.

"Anybody who wanted to swim before dinner, better go now," Mary Louise called. "The potatoes are just going on the barbecue."

Spring joined a laughing circle of old friends, and they went up to the house to change. A few minutes later they emerged. Penny wrinkled her nose and grinned at Spring.

"I never could get into swimming," she said easily. "I figure if I was meant to get into water any deeper than my bathtub, I would have been born with fins."

Reed was no longer with Penny, and Spring frowned slightly to see Penny's arm looped casually through Judd's. But that was just her way, Spring told herself. Penny had a big-city sophistication, and it seemed entirely natural that if an available man was nearby, Penny's arm would be through his.

Spring joined the group at the pool and found them choosing up teams for a water game. It was based loosely on water polo, and Spring was one of the first selected. She was a strong swimmer, and her reputation as a competitor hadn't been forgotten. Spring held nothing back in sports, always baffled and slightly irritated by girls who pretended to be weak and helpless at the expense of their teams.

The game was rather bruisingly physical as people fought good-naturedly over the ball, and Spring was enjoying herself immensely until, out of the corner of her eye, she spotted Reed poised on the edge of the pool. She had to fight with everything she had to restrain a gasp of pure admiration from escaping her. His awesome physique was certainly shown to best advantage in a brief set of close-fitting white swim trunks.

He stood there only a few moments, then dove cleanly into the water. The team Spring was playing against had been a man short, and they welcomed Reed in to their ranks. Spring and Reed had been swimming together in the lakes ever since she could remember, and her strong stroke was mostly thanks to his teaching. It soon emerged that they were the strongest swimmers, and to her dismay the captain of her team assigned her to guard Reed.

At first she was more restrained than she had been, but her natural competitive spirit and her involvement in the game won out. She was soon wresting the ball aggressively away from Reed, just as he was wresting it from her.

And before she knew it, she found herself laughing as she chased him across the pool, or as he chased her. Dunking was not only allowed but encouraged. Without hesitation Reed bullied her for the ball, using his superior strength and trying to intimidate her by pulling her under the water. She would surface gasping and hurl herself onto his broad frame until she had the satisfaction of submerging him.

Bit by bit, the less experienced swimmers crawled gasping from the pool, until Reed and Spring were the only ones left. She was so caught up in the music of his laughter that she barely noticed that they were the last ones left. All she knew was that she felt a wonderful, relaxed exhilaration that she hadn't felt with Reed in a long, long time.

Like young otters they dashed and ducked and raced, the air around them shivering merrily with the sound of their laughter. They splashed each other with the heels of their hands and struggled for possession of the ball. They squirmed and fought against the captivity of each other's arms as each tried to prevent the other from scoring a goal.

Slowly she became aware of an undercurrent between them—an unseen force trying to push powerfully through the almost childlike playfulness of their game. Spring was forced to acknowledge her awareness that the game masked a different enjoyment—the sensual pleasure of his hard, muscled body coming into contact with hers, his arms around her as he tried to reach for the ball, the colour of his eyes and the curling of his wet hair....

Suddenly she found herself snared in a bone-crushing hug that was intended to force her to release the ball from her stubborn hold.

"Reed!" She'd intended it to sound like a protest at his manhandling, but instead it came out faintly pleading, a whisper, and the pretense of the game was over.

The air tingled, charged, as her eyes locked with his and the smooth, wet surface of her skin pressed with slippery sensuality against the corded muscles of his nearly naked body. The sleek jersey fabric of her own bathing suit was molded to her like a second skin, giving her the strangest sensation of nudity and hiding nothing of her body's reaction to him. Oddly, she didn't feel self-conscious at all. Her fingers caressed the droplets of water clinging to the rugged, beloved surface of his face, and her arms moved to coil around his neck.

With a savage moan, which was part protest, part hunger, he surrendered to her helpless invitation and wrapped one arm solidly around her waist, drawing her even closer to the molten silk of his skin. The other hand wrapped itself in the tangled golden tresses of her hair and gently tugged, bringing her head back with insistence. She looked up at him with half-lidded eyes. Her lips faintly parted and unconsciously invited.

Reed moaned again, and his mouth came down on hers. There was no gentleness in him this time—he was not guardian, tutor or teacher. This time he was a man, and his lips demanded that she be a woman. The kiss was scorching and urgent. It touched something primal in her, and her response was feral and unfettered. A shuddering thrill raced through her, and she left the last traces of childhood behind her. This was what she wanted, this was what she was ready for. She pressed herself even closer to him, felt the wild beat of his heart and knew hers matched his identically. They were merging—their history, their misunderstandings, their differences were being melted by an inferno that dwarfed all else.

Dare to dream, she thought, not knowing where in her memory the phrase came from, but knowing this was her moment, this was the dream—the secret, hidden, haunting dream—coming true for her.

"Din-din, guys—unless you like your steaks on the leathery side, out you get."

At the sound of Penny's voice, Reed dropped Spring abruptly and for a moment Spring thought she was drowning, not in water, but in the waves and waves of agony that accompanied the breaking of her heart.

Her eyes flew to where Penny stood by the side of the pool and then to Reed's face. It was masked and casual, as if her moment had never existed beyond the walls of her imagination. She looked again at Penny. Maybe it hadn't happened, she thought, her mind still floating, unable to make the transition from the dream to reality.

Maybe none of it had been at all—not the look in his eyes, not the faintly savage, hugely enticing sensuality of his kiss. But even if it had been, it was no more. The moment of the kiss was gone, the edges turning hazy and hard to remember like a dream when one is startled awake.

He was watching her closely, and she saw the regret in his eyes even before he spoke.

"I'm sorry, Spring," he said softly.

Would he have reacted like that to any woman in a wet bathing suit who threw herself at him? Was that what he meant by he was sorry?

Sorry! She wanted to laugh, except that she knew the laughter would turn to tears. *Sorry for what, Reed? For responding to me like a man responds to a woman? For giving me the most joyous moment of my life? Or for seeing that I love you when you've already given your heart to another? Or just for the fact that she saw us?*

"Oh, bug off!" she exclaimed sharply, the sound of her voice exploding the last of the dream into a million scattered fragments. He winced, as though she'd struck him. Then his face became remote, and he hopped from the pool lithely. Penny looped a towel over his neck, her hands resting on both ends of it as she smiled up at him. He smiled back down, and Spring swung angrily away from the intimate little scene, got out of the pool and marched to the house, refusing to glance back.

Later she picked at her steak, trying hard to feign an appetite in front of her hosts but not succeeding. She glanced at Reed now and then. He was talking to Jimmy, thoroughly engrossed in a conversation about orchards and seemingly unperturbed by the incident in the pool, which he had probably already dismissed from his mind.

Penny was eating with Judd, laughing merrily as if she were unaware Reed was alive.

Dear Penny's plan B, Spring reminded herself bitterly, was to make Reed jealous, and did that go double if he'd just finished making her jealous?

When dinner had finally finished, Mary Louise addressed her guests. "Let's adjourn to the fire pit for some marshmallows and music. At great expense to the management, tonight's entertainment is an old-fashioned sing-along."

Night was starting to fall gently as Jimmy got the fire going, and the boisterous crowd gathered around the fire pit. Spring sat cross-legged on the ground, her guitar on her lap, willing herself not to look up when Reed joined her.

She sat stiffly beside him, tuning her guitar with more concentration than it required. But out of the corner of her eye she watched him and was more aware of him than she'd ever been—of his relaxed posture, of how the light played across his face when he bent over his twelve-string, of how he carefully listened to each note as he picked it. Then they tuned together, hardly speaking, listening instead to the notes of each other's guitars.

Reed began, his fingers moving skillfully down the cords of his guitar. He picked a lively folk tune that everybody knew, and soon hands were clapping and voices were following the confident lead of his.

Spring found herself struggling with her less complicated six-string. I'm out of practise, she told herself defensively, but she knew her struggles came from the painful picture that her mind insisted on recalling.

It was a picture of her and Reed sitting on the steps of the big house porch. On nights like this one, their heads were close together as he played a tune and then signalled her to try or covered her hands with his and led her through each step of a new song.

"Sing something together," Mary Louise called out. The crowd applauded their approval, and Spring tried not to cringe. She let out an inward sigh of relief when Reed suggested a light and lively little tune, and not one of those romantic ballads that lent themselves so well to a duet.

At first her voice wavered in the shadow of his, but then she closed her eyes, letting herself go, and her voice came flowing out of her, harmonizing naturally with his. Soaring above it, then intermingling with it. When they finished, there was an awed silence before the applause.

Reed moved on quickly, singing folk songs, ballads and the music of Canadian favorites.

Finally Spring looked at her fingers and stretched them ruefully. She set down her guitar and made her excuses with an apologetic smile.

She got herself a few marshmallows and toasted them over the fire as she listened to Reed and watched him out of the corner of her eye. He cut a rather romantic figure with the firelight softening the features of his face and his strong voice emerging confidently from the others. But finally, he, too, said he'd had enough.

"One more," Mary Louise pleaded. "Reed, do the spring song."

Spring felt herself stiffen, then hastily concentrated on her marshmallow.

There was an awkward pause. "I don't think so," Reed refused quietly.

"The spring song?"

Spring recognized Penny's voice and looked over at her. Her eyes widened when she saw that she was nestled comfortably in the curve of Judd's arms and that their hands were interlocked. The plot of plan B thickens, Spring thought caustically.

"Reed wrote it for Spring when she was just little," Mary Louise explained. "She had the mumps, and she was in bed complaining about missing the blossoms. Reed wrote this little song to bring spring in to her. Or maybe," she said slyly, "it was about her. He never said for sure."

"Oh, Reed, please sing it," Penny pleaded.

"Yes, Reed, please. I haven't heard it for so long," Mrs. K added persuasively.

He hesitated, and Spring was aware of his eyes on her. He shrugged and began to pick out a dancing, fast-paced melody. His eyes sought hers again, and this time he watched her intently as he began to sing.

"Spring comes a-dancing
She opens the door....
Her smile is the sunshine,
And it's winter no more.

Spring comes a-laughing
A-laughing out loud....
Her breath the warm breezes
That lift winter's shroud.

Spring comes a-giving
A-giving to me...
The fragrance of the flowers
And the humming of the bees."

He broke off there, playing his guitar with flying fingers, unleashing the spirit of spring with his music as accurately as a writer might do with words, a painter with watercolours. The melody was at once light and lively, hopeful and high-spirited. It conjured up visions of sudden storms and bright skies, of the apple blossoms and of newborn foals flicking their heels toward the sun. Then Reed repeated the same melody, only this time slower, with subtle variations in it. It became sadness mingled with joy almost so that they could not be told apart. His eyes still on her face, he sang the last verse, his deep voice mirroring the mood of the music.

"Spring leaves a-dancing,
She closes the door;
But her magic, it lingers...
And it's spring evermore."

For a moment the silence was complete and Spring was aware of a dozen pairs of eyes fastened on her face. And then they clapped for Reed, and he acknowledged the applause with a slightly self-mocking bow of his head and put down his guitar.

People drifted toward the patio, where the stereo speakers were being set up for dancing, but Spring continued to sit by the fire, staring unseeingly into the flames, the little melody playing over and over again in her head.

Mary Louise appeared out of the darkness and sat down beside Spring. "Maybe I shouldn't have asked him to play that one, hmm?" she commented, regarding Spring thoughtfully.

"It doesn't matter," Spring said dully.

"Didn't you see the way he looked at you when he was singing it?" Mary Louise demanded impatiently.

"Two can play by plan B," Spring muttered.

"Plan B?" Mary Louise echoed.

Would Reed do that? Spring wondered bleakly. Would he really sing her song to make another woman jealous? Of course, it hadn't been his idea to sing the song, but once pressed, who could blame him for taking advantage of an opportunity like that? Especially with Penny all cuddled up into Judd at the time?

Penny didn't have an ounce of sense, Spring decided blackly. Really, if you wanted to make a man like Reed jealous, you would have to pick someone a little more awe inspiring than poor old Judd, nice as he was.

Mary Louise nudged her. "Come join the party," she insisted, and though her heart wasn't in it, Spring agreed. She danced every dance, but her popularity didn't impress her at all. It was a strain trying to pretend that she was enjoying herself.

A slow, romantic waltz came on, and she was a little startled to find herself in Reed's arms. She held herself stiffly and formally apart from him, resisting the light pressure that he put on the small of her back to draw her closer.

And for all that, she still had to admit that Reed was the only man she ever felt totally comfortable dancing with. With others, she always had to keep track of what she was doing—counting out a tedious one-two-three-one inside her head. But with Reed, the count was forgotten, and the exercise became effortless as he guided her smoothly over the patio dance floor.

"Penny says you don't look happy tonight," Reed commented, breaking the silence between them.

"Did she?" Spring responded coolly. "Did she think it might cheer me up if you danced with me?" Say no, she pleaded inwardly. Reed, please tell me this was your idea.

But he refused to either confirm or deny her suspicion; he only continued to gaze at her thoughtfully. Angrily, she broke away from his grasp and stalked off the dance floor, making her way to the house.

She was in the kitchen pretending a need for a new soft drink when Penny flounced in. Her cheeks were flaming with high colour, and her eyes held the most beautiful sparkling light in them.

It must have come from flirting outrageously with two men, Spring deduced, having noted that Penny seemed to be dividing her time fairly evenly between Judd and Reed.

"Spring, it's working. I almost can't believe it, but it's working!"

"What's working?" Spring asked, not even troubling to pretend interest.

Penny looked at her as if she'd lost her mind, then laughed. "Silly—plan B!"

"Wonderful," Spring said dully. "Just wonderful."

Penny didn't seem to notice Spring's lack of enthusiasm. Instead, she hugged herself and looked impossibly dreamy.

"Reed sees the writing on the wall."

"Does he?" Spring forced herself to ask.

"You know what he said?" Penny didn't wait for Spring's reply. "He said he's thinking of building a house on the old cabin site. It has to be for us, Spring. Don't you think so?"

Spring thought she was close to fainting, but she managed to compose herself. "What's wrong with the old house?" she asked stiffly.

Penny looked at her oddly and laughed again. "Spring, I know I said that I wanted us to be like sisters, but that would be taking the concept of one big, happy family just a step too far, don't you think?"

Of course, Spring thought dizzily, the two newlyweds wouldn't want to share accommodations with anyone else. They'd want their own little love nest. Reed had worked it all out. Rather than ask her to leave again, he'd just build a new house for his bride. Was he that insensitive to her feelings that he thought she'd stay after he had married Penny?

"Couldn't you be just a little happy for me, Spring?" Penny asked her softly, her large dark eyes puzzled and hurt.

Spring remembered her resolve to let Reed go his own way and to never let him know why she would go her way. She supposed now was as good a time as any to start setting the stage.

"Of course I'm happy for you, Penny," she said huskily. "I think you're a very good couple."

"Oh, dear," Penny said with a small laugh. "I'm out of line. I'm trying to force congratulations out of you, and he hasn't even asked me the question yet. But I'm not completely out of my mind—I know I'm not. Even Mrs. K was saying tonight she could hear wedding bells, and she's uncanny at sensing stuff like that. And she knows him better than just about anybody else, so..."

Spring felt bitterly betrayed by the fact that Mrs. K was predicting Penny and Reed's wedding. *She also knows me better than just about anybody else,* Spring thought. *Doesn't she know how I feel about him—what this is going to do to me? Doesn't she care?*

Feeling lonely and lost, Spring couldn't force herself into a party mood. She did force herself back onto the patio, but only long enough to pretend a headache and get the keys to Reed's car so that she could go home.

Halfway home, she realized the lovebirds would be forced to share a ride with Judd and Mrs. K. She hoped, with small and grim satisfaction, that it would limit their good-night kiss. She grinned a tight and humourless smile—knowing suddenly what it felt like to tilt at windmills.

Chapter Nine

It was only two days later when Penny came in the back door without knocking. The men were already in the orchard, and she stood facing Mrs. K and Spring. Her lips trembled and her eyes shone with the most incredible lustre, betraying unshed tears.

"What is it, dear?" Mrs. K asked with surprised concern.

Penny opened and closed her mouth several times, then began to cry and laugh at the same time. "He asked," she finally choked out, her whole face lighting up even as the tears rolled unchecked down her cheeks. "He asked me to marry him," she whispered with stunned wonder.

Mrs. K bounced across the kitchen and engulfed Penny in one of her bony hugs. "Oh, my gosh," she said over and over again, her tears joining Penny's as they clung to each other, laughing and weeping. "I'm so happy, Penny. You've made me so happy. I love both of you so much."

Spring's coffee cup slid from oddly numb fingers, crashed to the table and shattered. Mrs. K and Penny whirled and stared at her, and then Penny broke from the embrace and rushed over.

"Spring, are you cut? My God, you're whiter than a ghost. Are you going to faint?"

Spring managed to shake her head and forced herself to concentrate on the spreading brown puddle she was methodically wiping up with her napkin. She almost wished she was cut—it would give her an excuse to release the storm of tears gathering pressure behind her lashes.

With Herculean effort she gathered her wits and smiled shakily at Penny. "Congratulations," she murmured. In her own ears her voice sounded strained and brittle to the breaking point.

The concern in Penny's eyes did not diminish. "Are you sure you're okay?"

"Fine," Spring said woodenly, hoping the grimace on her face would pass for a smile. She busied herself collecting shards of glass, refusing to meet those large, worried brown eyes. A strained silence fell. Mrs. K shrugged a shoulder helplessly toward Penny's puzzled look at Spring turned to deposit the broken coffee mug in the garbage beneath the sink.

"Here comes the man of the hour now," Mrs. K announced, obviously relieved that a counterpoint was being provided to the fine and baffling tension that had invaded her kitchen.

Spring heard his footstep on the stairs, and then the door creaked open and his shadow fell across her shoulders before she could even attempt a mad dash for freedom. How could she face him? What could she possibly say? She froze, refusing for a moment to turn and look at him. She closed her eyes, fighting for composure, struggling to suppress the pain, the anguished sadness that was filling her like floodwater, seeping relentlessly into every crevice and crack of her being, leaving nothing untouched.

Finally, with her eyes lowered and barely breathing, she turned from the protection of the sink. It took all her strength, every ounce of courage she possessed, to lift her eyes.

Judd Black stood in the doorway.

Spring's mouth fell open. Her heart seemed to begin to beat again, fluttering like a tremulous bird on the wings of hope. Was it possible...? No, Reed must be right behind Judd. It would be cruel to allow herself to believe—no, not just cruel, it could kill her.

And then the expression on Judd's face managed to pierce even the foggy and frantic whirlings of her mind. He was leaning against the door frame, his eyes riveted on Penny's shining face. A boyish smile of pure wonder played across his lips. Spring looked at Penny. The two of them—Judd and Penny—stood absolutely motionless, locked in the warm and golden embrace that shone out of each of their eyes.

The spell broke, and Penny dashed into Judd's arms. "I couldn't wait," she confessed laughingly. "I told them."

Spring stared at them, dazed. Penny and Judd? The homespun farmboy and the big-city sophisticate? Craggy earthiness and porcelain perfection? Fire and water? Who would have ever guessed at this unlikely combination? The possibility had never even entered her mind.

But now, studying them, she wondered why it hadn't. Perhaps the combination wasn't as unlikely as it first appeared. Though in many ways it was an attraction of op-

posites, their differences would complement each other—
his calm and her high-spiritedness. But in deeper ways
there was a sameness, a gentleness and lovingness of nature that made them seem very well suited.

"Think she should have her head examined?" Judd
asked Spring lightly.

Spring laughed out loud, partly out of sheer happiness for Penny and Judd, but mostly because of the sudden release from the terrible strain she'd been under.
"You're the one who should have your head examined," she reproached Judd, "for holding out for so
long."

"Anything worth having is worth fighting for," Penny
quipped, but Spring got the impression she was being
looked at meaningfully.

"Did I even have a chance?" Judd asked with mock
indignation.

"No," Penny assured him easily, "you didn't."

Spring could contain herself no longer. She crossed to
them, stood on tiptoe to plant a kiss on Judd's cheek and
turned to envelop Penny in a hug every bit as vigorous as
the one Mrs. K had subjected her to.

"Oh, Penny," Spring confessed softly. "I made the
worst mistake. You won't believe what I thought. I owe
you an apology. You see, I thought—" She stopped,
feeling awkwardly afraid of revealing too much.

Penny's eyes widened and understanding dawned in
them. "Oh, no," she breathed compassionately. "You
thought . . . ?" And then she, too, stopped, cautious of
revealing too much.

Mrs. K was regarding them both with interest. "What
kind of code are you two talking in?" she demanded
mildly.

Penny slipped her arm around Spring's waist and gave her a squeeze, reassuring her that the secret was safe. "We're not talking in a code," she denied. "We're just on the same wavelength—a little bit like sisters."

She and Spring exchanged a glance deep with understanding and affection. It was in that moment that Spring knew who Penny reminded her of.

Later that afternoon Spring sat by the creek, idly stirring the cool, gurgling water with her bare feet. Penny didn't love Reed. Reed didn't love Penny. It struck her that she should be overjoyed by that discovery, yet she wasn't. Instead she felt gravely troubled.

How could she have been so blindly and stupidly oblivious to the fact that it was Judd Black that Penny had her heart set on? It was true they were an unlikely couple, yet Spring knew it was unlike herself to judge things superficially. She should have picked up on the deeper similarities between them. And now that she *knew*, it was so easy to recall dozens of clues that any reasonably intelligent human being would have picked up on with ease. How could she have missed the wistfulness in Judd's eyes the week Penny had worked in the orchard? Or the sparkling vivaciousness that came to Penny when Judd was near? Of course, the electricity and tenderness between them hadn't come completely out in the open until they'd announced their engagement this morning, but still Spring believed she should have caught on. She had refused to see it. Why?

Understanding hit her unexpectedly, shattering through her like a bolt of lightning ripping across a night sky. In some deep, unadmitted part of herself she had linked Reed and Penny together because she believed Penny was every bit the woman that Reed deserved as a wife. She had spirit, warmth, charm, beauty and maturity. But the illumination was painful because it went deeper still. Reluctantly she wove in the final thread. All along Penny had reminded her of someone. But it was only this morning, when she'd finally allowed herself to respond to Penny's affectionate nature, that she knew who that someone was.

Dee Caldwell, Reed's mother. Penny reminded her of Dee. Spring wondered how long she had subconsciously fought off making the connection between those two women. Their similarities were hardly physical, and yet they were striking, nonetheless. They both possessed an inborn grace, a complete and natural confidence in their sheer femininity.

Dee. Spring felt a pang of loneliness at having recalled the woman she had loved and admired above all others. She recalled the strength and maturity behind those laughter-filled eyes, the aura of class that even rare appearances in jeans and gardening gloves didn't dispell— just as Penny would be no less glamourous dressed as a scarecrow. Both women were at ease in the fullness of their womanhood.

Spring sighed heavily. Dee had died before passing on the secret of her innate grace, before passing on very much at all. Mrs. K was good-hearted, of course, but hopelessly outdated as far as providing a coach to help Spring as she journeyed that steep, long road to maturity.

It was a void that Spring hadn't even been aware of until now. She felt woefully insecure about the skills that had eluded her because she had been so absorbed in the masculine world of Reed and her father.

There was an irony in that. She had been able to excuse Reed's lack of interest in her when she'd linked him to Penny. But now Spring had to face the painful fact that though most of her youth had been influenced by men, she was unprepared to deal with them in the typically feminine sense.

Like Reed's reaction to her in the swimming pool—had she been more knowledgeable, she might have been able to discern whether he was motivated by pure physical chemistry or whether there was genuine interest involved. If a wet female form simply called forth a certain purely physical reaction, that would certainly explain his apology—since Penny no longer provided an explanation.

She sighed again, even more heavily. And if she didn't possess the feminine insight to even know when a man was interested in her, she was even less knowledgeable about how to let a man know she was interested in him. Basic flirting and coquetry skills had passed her by entirely.

Her list grew under her savage self-examination. She lacked the usual feminine interest in clothing, jewelry, perfumes, hairstyles and cosmetic trends. And her domestic skills extended about as far as making a peanut butter sandwich or frying an egg.

No, she decided grimly, she was not exactly a shining example of womanhood. Somewhere along the way, because she loved Reed so, she had paired him with a woman who was all the things a woman was *supposed* to be—just as he was all the things a man was supposed to be. No wonder he had shown only brotherly interest in her—except for the occasional chemical slip, which was dictated more by the physical proximity of the circumstances than any deeper feeling, she was certain.

Maybe those flashes of chemical attraction did give her something to work with. After all, you did have to have that, too, to have a well-rounded relationship. Penny's words of this morning came back to her: "Anything worth having is worth fighting for."

And Reed was worth having. Oh, Lord, he was worth having. But how would she begin to fight when she didn't even have the weapons?

A spark of hope leapt in her. What was to say she couldn't learn the skills that would make her the ideal wife for Reed? If she would have chosen something else to do with her life, had chosen to become a doctor, lawyer or teacher, she'd have had to learn the skills to make the dream a reality. Why did she think being the woman Reed deserved should be any less an ambition?

Smiling, she withdrew her feet from the creek. Hadn't she even taken that bookkeeping course in anticipation—however deeply she had hidden her motives, even from herself—that it would be useful to her on the orchard? Well, she certainly proved that she wasn't stupid, and now she planned to direct her intelligence in a different direction. A bookkeeper was obviously not what Reed was looking for in a woman!

She hopped up and grimaced wryly down at herself. Her faded jeans were rolled up past her knees, her T-shirt was shapeless from too many washings and the sneakers she jammed her wet feet into had definitely seen a better day.

Good God in heaven! she berated herself. She was a twenty-one year old *woman*. Why was she dressed like a ten-year old going out to play street ball? Well, that was going to change.

"Did I even have a chance?" Judd had asked Penny this morning.

"No," she had replied with absolute confidence, "you didn't."

"And neither do you, Reed Caldwell," Spring murmured wickedly to herself.

That first flush of confidence had faded somewhat by the following morning. In fact, Spring was feeling exceedingly self-conscious by the time she walked into the kitchen. She had chosen her sky-blue sundress, remembering the reaction it had elicited before, and she had also put on makeup, something she usually only bothered with on special occasions. She'd had to apply it three times to get just the natural effect she wanted; consequently, Reed was done with breakfast by the time she appeared in the kitchen.

He was lingering over coffee, reading the newspaper, and he glanced up at her. "Going somewhere?" he asked casually, his eyes already back scanning the paper.

"No," she snapped defensively, getting a coffee and taking the seat across from him.

"Well, don't bite my head off," he said calmly. "I just asked a question. Get up on the wrong side of the bed?"

She glared at him disbelievingly. He was supposed to be enraptured with her fresh, feminine appearance, and instead he asked if she got out on the wrong side of the bed! She had to bite her lip to keep herself from yelling a very ungraceful "Drop dead" at him.

Reed finished off his coffee, folded his paper and got up. "Have a nice day, sugar," he said absently.

"Don't call me that!" His use of her childish nickname grated unbearably after all her efforts.

His eyebrows rose in surprise. "I thought you liked it," he reminded her softly.

"I don't like being treated like a child," she informed him stiffly.

"Then don't act like one," he suggested, his patience thinning. He turned and left, letting the screen door slam behind him.

Spring put her elbows on the table and cupped her face in the palms of her hands. She had the most childish urge to stamp her foot—or to cry.

Her frustration of that morning multiplied itself over the next week. Each day she dressed as carefully and attractively as she knew how. She had even slipped into town to add a few feminine dresses and blouses to a wardrobe that she now recognized as being distinctly tomboyish.

The second day was even worse than the first. Reed took in her attire without even attempting to hide his bafflement. "I won't even ask," he muttered.

The third day his eyes swept her, taking in the satin-blend, cream-coloured pantsuit and the matching earrings. He made no comment whatsoever. His mouth tightened, and his eyes darkened to a green that looked vaguely angry. After that, he seemed to become totally indifferent, his eyes unreadable and hooded before he buried himself behind his paper each morning.

She stubbornly stuck to her plan. One of these days, Reed was going to be forced to acknowledge that she'd blossomed into womanhood and was no longer that grubby little elf he had rescued from the orchard fifteen years ago. It was discouraging to come face-to-face with how much he seemed to want to avoid that moment.

There were other discouraging factors to her self-education though she was anxious to avoid admitting them. Her clothes were lovely and attractive. They were also restrictive. She couldn't just dash outside and go for a walk. She had to change to work in the garden. She didn't feel she could offer to help with the chores. She couldn't fling herself into the creek when the midday heat became unbearable because the makeup that it took her nearly an hour to apply would wash off or run in unbecoming black streaks down her face.

She was beginning to feel like a very pretty—and useless—little doll. Or like a little girl dressed up for Sunday school, then placed in a corner with the firm instruction not to move, not to get dirty—not to live!

But Dee Caldwell had almost always worn a dress, Spring reminded herself sternly. It had never seemed to bother her. She'd never seemed to notice how impractical and totally bothersome it was. Obviously, Spring deduced, she was having problems because she was cultivating the look and not the life-style. Without much enthusiasm, she decided that she'd better start to explore some ladylike interests to keep her mind from constantly yearning to be outside.

"Spring, what are you doing?" Reed's tone was incredulous.

Spring quickly unclamped her tongue from between her teeth and smiled—with what she hoped was domestic tranquility—at Reed. He was standing in the doorway to the living room, his chest bare and enticingly bronze in contrast to the white towel slung around his neck.

He looked marvelously masculine, and her heart leapt within her. If she could only convince him to see her as as much a woman as he was a man!

"I'm knitting," she told him demurely.

He stared at her. "Are you nuts? Have you gone completely crazy? It's a hundred and four degrees in the shade, and you're buried under twenty pounds of wool?"

Her smile became slightly strained and must not have hidden her hurt from those alert eyes.

He crossed the room and looked down at her. "Come for a dip in the creek," he suggested, his tone gentle and inviting.

She closed her eyes momentarily to gather strength. He was ready to go—she would have to wash off a layer of cosmetics, and then carefully reapply it. Plus, she wasn't sure if cavorting in the creek went with her new image. All her hard work could go down the tubes if she gave in to the temptation of a delightfully childish frolic in the swimming hole.

"No thanks," she said brightly, though her teeth were clenched.

Reed frowned down at her, his eyes searching. A lean, tanned finger touched her cheek.

"You're starting to look as pale and washed out as an old dishrag, Spring. You need to get outside more."

Her knitting hit the ground with a thud as she abruptly stood up, her hands clenched at her sides to prevent her from hitting him. *How dare he?* After all she had gone through, after all she was doing...

"You are an insulting, intolerable, despicable example of the human species and—"

"And you hate me," he finished mockingly, laughter-filled gaze dancing across her flushed, outraged face. "That's better," he said with satisfaction, turned and strode, whistling, out the door.

Her hands closed around a vase on the end table beside her.

Reed popped his head back in the door. "Throw it," he suggested mildly. "You'll feel better."

She set down the vase with haughty self-restraint. Reed shrugged and disappeared.

She glared after him. He had manipulated her into a childish display of temper with infuriating ease! Her plan was not working! At all! She stomped into the kitchen, badly in need of advice. She picked up a bowl of peas off the counter and began to shell them furiously.

"Mrs. K," she said, the casual note in her voice forced, "did you ever notice that Dee Caldwell had a quality about her of—well, grace?"

Mrs. K smiled with fond remembrance and did not seem to find anything the least suspicious about the question. "Everybody who knew Dee noticed that quality."

"How do you suppose she got like that?" Spring asked conversationally. "Is that what a finishing school does? Gives a person that kind of nice polish?"

Mrs. K looked at Spring with astonishment. "My dear, Dee never went to finishing school. She was straight out of the backwoods, Dee was." Mrs. K laughed gently. "You should have seen her the first few years she was married—as awkward as a long-legged colt, shy, gauche—"

"Dee!" Spring squeaked. "But then how did she ever become—"

"Such a lady?" Mrs. K's expression became faraway. "It wasn't anything she seemed to work at doing. Just every year she'd evolve a bit, grow a little more confident, a little more sure of herself. Comes from being loved by a man like Bob, I always thought. He cherished her, Spring. He never asked her to be something that she wasn't and because of that, she became the best she could be. Oh, and how she loved that man, too. Those two could just look at each other, and the whole room would light up. And what they felt for each other seemed to touch every single person they met and every single thing they did. I never tried to put words to it before, but you said it just fine. A quality of grace. I like that."

Spring threw several empty pods in with the shelled peas, and several peas into the bowl for the discarded pods. If Mrs. K was correct, then she was in an impossible bind. She needed a man to love her to achieve that elusive quality of grace, but she had already decided she needed grace to get that man to love her.

Mrs. K came over and looked at the bowls. "Why don't you go outside?" she asked with faint exasperation.

"I don't want to," Spring said. Her tone became unconsciously self-mocking. "It's very hard on the complexion."

"I think maybe you're going about this the wrong way," Mrs. K said with gentle hesitation.

Spring stiffened. "Going about what?"

Mrs. K sighed. "You know...."

"I don't!" Still, her colour deepened a few shades.

"Spring, just be yourself," Mrs. K advised awkwardly.

Spring saw how well-intentioned the advice was and patted Mrs. K reassuringly on the hand. "I will," she promised out loud, but inwardly she moaned, *As soon as I find out who that is.* And at the moment, she had to admit, she felt farther from finding herself than she had ever felt before.

Chapter Ten

On Saturday afternoon, Spring slipped into the kitchen. "I thought I might cook dinner since it's your bridge night," she announced casually to Mrs. K.

Mrs. K didn't turn from the sink. "Not much point, since only you and Reed will be—oh." She turned and looked at Spring and her mouth fell open with shock. "What have you done, love?" she asked softly.

Spring ran self-conscious fingers through the short feathered wisps of hair that had replaced her long, heavy tresses. "I had my hair cut," she said with a lightness that denied the tears of loss she had cried most of the way home. She had tried to convince herself the cut was chic; it did make her look more sophisticated, and more importantly, her age.

"I can see that," Mrs. K said dryly. "Why?"

"Just for a change." Just because she had thought a startling new haircut might be the dramatic touch needed to shake Reed into awareness of the woman she was becoming. That, coupled with a romantic dinner for two...

Mrs. K sighed and made no further comment on the haircut. "I'd keep dinner simple if I were you. It's too hot for a heavy meal."

Spring glared at her. Simplicity was not what she had in mind, and she suspected the advice was addressed more at her lack of experience than the heat. For goodness' sake, anybody who could read and follow instructions could cook!

Later she ruefully admitted it wasn't quite that easy. The counters were cluttered with dirty dishes. There was flour on the floor and a stray noodle or two fried to the top of the stove. Still, her Beef Tenderloin Bourguignon simmered quietly on the stove and smelled heavenly.

She glanced at the clock. The mess would have to wait. She charged up to her room and slipped into a lovely dress of white Indian cotton with a sheared top and string straps. It managed to look both casual and exceedingly feminine at the same time. Then she turned hastily to her mirror and felt sudden weariness engulf her.

What was the use? she asked herself dejectedly. Even the startling new haircut and a ton of cosmetics weren't going to hide *that* look. She had been noticing it in herself for several days—a wan, strained cast to her features, a shadowed sadness about her eyes. Wearily, she wondered what she really wanted. Sometimes, these days, she felt she wasn't even sure. What if she succeeded in winning Reed through all this effort and sacrifice? Would she then have to play a role she wasn't particularly comfortable with for the rest of her life? Wouldn't it be the most painful of shams if Reed fell in love with something she was not?

I'm not being phony, she defended herself heatedly. I'm only trying to learn and grow. But a little voice inside of her wouldn't let it rest.

Growth, it informed her, *is always authentic. You grow when you go in the directions your heart leads you. You shrivel up and die when you try to force yourself into molds you have no real desire to fit into.*

"But I do have a real desire to be a full woman," Spring wailed defensively. Firmly, she pulled herself away from her self-defeating introspection, squared her shoulders and marched downstairs. She laid the dining room table with the finest lace cloth, Wedgwood china and the heavy, antique silver. She hesitated for just a moment before adding candles, then sat down to admire the sheer artistry of her table. The feeling of exhaustion—she was certainly not going to admit it might be depression—returned and washed over her.

She rested her head on her arms. Everything was done. Reed should be up from the orchard in a few minutes. It wouldn't hurt to shut her eyes for a few seconds....

"What the hell—it's like a blast furnace in here!"

Spring jerked awake as the front door slammed behind Reed. She looked sleepily through the archway to see him standing in the hall. It shouldn't be this dark, she realized, even as she saw him tense. She smelled smoke at the same time as she noticed it hanging wispily in the shadows of the room.

She bolted from her chair and arrived in the kitchen only a fraction of a second behind Reed. He unceremoniously grabbed her smoking creation off the stove, dumped it in the sink and turned on the faucet.

She remained in the shadows. "I was going to surprise you," she said tremulously.

"You succeeded," he muttered over his shoulder as he cranked open the window above the sink.

"It's because you're late," she said with halfhearted accusation, glancing at the clock.

"I was having trouble with the irrigation system in block C." He looked blandly around the mess in the kitchen, and then his eyes drifted to the dining room door. He gazed thoughtfully at her carefully laid table, and for the first time his eyes sought her.

They narrowed, the table and the mess in the kitchen obviously dismissed, and she tried to push farther back into the shadows. He crossed the kitchen in a single stride and caught her shoulders painfully, his eyes raking her. With a muttered oath, he released her, reached behind her and flipped on the light. It flooded the room mercilessly, and he stared at her.

There was no startled awareness in his eyes. He was not looking at her with the dawning understanding she had hoped and prayed for. His expression was pained—as if she were a six-year-old who had indiscriminately and gleefully hacked off her hair with a pair of blunt-nosed scissors.

"Spring," he finally whispered, "Oh, Spring." He reached out and touched the blunt fronds of hair that framed her face with an oddly caressing hand. "Your beautiful, beautiful hair," he said with a trace of mourning in his voice. "What have you done? Why?"

She didn't trust herself to speak. It had been such a sacrifice to cut off her beloved hair. She had loved it long and heavy, had loved the touch of it against her shoulders, had loved to feel fingers of wind playing through it, lifting it from her face. It had been a sacrifice. It had been a gift for him, and it had failed. Her gaze skittered around the smoky kitchen. Just as each of her attempts had failed. The horrible truth was that she was a failure as a woman.

"What's gotten into you, Spring?" His voice was not so much accusing as sad. "When you first came home everything seemed to be fine. I thought I might find you changed—a stranger I no longer knew. But you weren't. You were everything I remembered, like sunshine bursting through the clouds. But now you're not. It's like something is dying inside of you. Every day you seem to become more of a stranger to me. Why?"

There was an oddly tortured note in his voice but she barely heard it. All she heard was a confirmation of what she'd already deduced. She was a failure.

She looked at her hands, not daring to speak, not even daring to look into those deep and gentle jade eyes and see the compassion and pity he felt for her.

He took her chin and forced her to look at him, his eyes scanning her face with unwanted sympathy.

He released her chin and looked again around the kitchen and through the doorway into the dining room. He glanced at her, taking in the defeated look and trying not to wince at the sight of her hair.

He changed tacts, wrapping a brotherly arm around her slumped shoulder. "Let's go outside and roast some hot dogs," he suggested quietly, a trace of a smile in his voice that he managed to keep off his face. "It'll give the house a chance to air out."

She jerked out from beneath the comforting weight of his arm. Didn't he understand anything? It was all wrong! Tonight she had wanted to dazzle him with sophistication. Tonight she had wanted to rid him of the childhood images he held on to—not reinforce them. Couldn't he see she was not dressed to go out and sit on a log and roast hot dogs over a fire?

She gambled. "Why don't you take me out for dinner?" she suggested huskily.

He frowned, hesitated. "Sure," he finally said. "If that's what you really want—"

She felt herself crumpling under his hesitation. He did not see her as the type of woman that he would wine and dine romantically. She crumpled further when she came face-to-face with the realization that it wasn't what she really wanted anyway. She honestly would enjoy spending an easy evening with him sitting by the fire, eating hot dogs, laughing, talking and maybe later playing their guitars together under the winking stars.

It was finally too much. She was caught in the web of her own self-deception, and she felt as unhappy and confused as she had ever felt in her life. It *was* a lie. It didn't matter that she'd tried to convince herself she was growing and learning. The whole thing was just a pretense—a disgusting pretense. She just couldn't be the type of woman he needed, wanted and deserved.

"Never mind," she managed to choke out, the tears filming her eyes. He reached for her but with a strangled sob she evaded his grasp, ran by him and dashed up the stairs.

He started after her, then stopped and stood very still, agonized. Even from where he stood he could hear her muffled, heart-wrenching sobs. Feeling old and defeated, he slumped down at the table and helplessly stared at his big hands.

She was through with artifice, Spring decided with determination. She looked at her puffy eyes, black-ringed after a nearly sleepless night, and shrugged. So be it. She pulled on her jeans and a plain but comfortable cotton blouse. But the battle was not yet over. She had one final move to make.

She was going to tell him. She was sick to death of trying to hide her feelings, of trying to win him over by being someone she was not. She was going to be honest and simply tell him the truth. That she loved him, that she had always loved him, that she would always love him. It was time to get it out in the open. Then the ball would be in his court. She was weary of second-guessing, hoping and trying to discern what was behind those hooded eyes. If he didn't return the feeling—her heart fell at the very thought, but her shoulders squared—it would hurt, it would hurt more than being boiled in oil, but at least she would know where she stood. She was young and strong, and though she severely doubted she would ever fully recover, she would at least be able to get on with her life—such as it might be without Reed in it. What was the alternative? To sit around here until she was old and grey, wishing, dreaming and praying?

Even though her mind was set irrevocably on its course, her heart was hammering in her throat as she went down the stairs. She entered the kitchen, and her heart sank when only Mrs. K was there. Would she ever be able to work up this kind of courage and determination again?

"Where's Reed?" she asked firmly. She would track him down if need be.

"He went to Kelowna on business this morning."

"Oh hell," she muttered.

"Pardon?"

"Nothing."

"Thanks for leaving everything so neat and tidy last night."

Spring looked at Mrs. K with surprise. Sarcasm was hardly her style. And then she realized it wasn't sarcasm. She peeked into the dining room. The table had been cleared, and the dishes put away. Reed. Had he recognized her pain and been trying to erase the nightmare for her? His seeming sensitivity sent a small hope dancing across her heart.

The day passed with unsettling slowness, even if it was such a joy to be outside again. She spent most of the day down at the swimming hole, dashing in and out for dips, and trying to pretend interest in the magazine she had brought. But the enormity of what she was planning to do kept creeping into her thoughts, and her stomach would begin to flip-flop nervously. She was determined not to rehearse what she would say, and not to try to project what his reaction might be, so she stubbornly kept turning pages.

As it turned out, it was just as well she had not prepared a speech because she had no chance to give it.

He came in late for dinner, greeted them all curtly, sat down without looking at her and ate his meal in surly silence. Her courage failed. There was something chillingly familiar in the remote, hard cast of his face.

"Spring, I want you to come into the office for a minute." His tone was indifferent and glacial. She followed him, trying to fight a crushing sense of déjà vu.

He stood with his powerful back to her, looking out the window. "The envelope on the desk is for you," he finally said in a clipped, cold voice.

She hesitated, wanting to run from the ice-edge in his voice, from the stranger he had become. She forced herself, instead, to reach for the envelope. She hesitated again, a premonition of dread stirring inside her, and then opened the envelope with clumsy, trembling fingers.

The room seemed to fade and blur, and she drew in a ragged breath to steady herself. She wished she could feel hate for him but found she couldn't. She had only herself to blame. Hadn't she known all along the risk involved in loving this man? She fingered the airline ticket to Vancouver for a long time before she spoke.

She had a choice now. She could fling herself at him wailing, weeping and pleading—she could follow through on her plan to tell him that she loved him. But it was all too much like it had been once before. Suddenly and sadly, she knew she had been presented with her opportunity to show grace, to cling to some small shred of dignity in her defeat.

"Why?" she finally managed, grimly satisfied with her soft composure.

He turned then, his face schooled into impassive lines. "I'm not quite the monster you think I am, Spring. I won't keep you here when it so obviously makes you unhappy. I have no right to keep you from what you want, and it's been pretty obvious that you're yearning for the bright lights. A place where you can wear your nice clothes, and go out—"

He stopped, and the cool jade of his eyes dropped from hers. He fingered some papers on his desk as if he were eager to get this over with and get on to new business.

His eyes lifted again, and his voice was flat and emotionless. "I should have never forced you to come back here. I should have realized the orchard—this lazy, little backwater—" his smile was grim "—wouldn't have anything to offer you anymore. I made a mistake. I'm sorry. I hope you'll forgive me."

She stared at him. He was so calm, so cool, so collected. He had marched back into her life, made her yearn as she had never yearned and dream as she had never dreamed. Now she was being dismissed as a casual error.

She could tell him, of course, that he had misunderstood the reasons for her unhappiness. But she would have to admit too much, and a ghost of the past haunted her. Had he really misunderstood, or did he understand too well? The courage she had felt earlier today was completely gone, and she could not make herself vulnerable to him—not again. Not ever again.

Wasn't this her answer, anyway? If he loved her he could not do this to her. If he loved her, even the tiniest little bit, he would be incapable of sending her away.

Her face as frozen as his, she looked again to the ticket. Tomorrow afternoon. He had lost no time in correcting his "error."

Numbly, wordlessly, she turned away from him. Her head high with pride, she walked out the door.

It was well past midnight when she crept out onto the coolness of the porch. Her room had been too closed, too confining. A bright moon washed the world silver—remarkably like the day she had come back home.

She stood staring out across the yard to the barn, a black hulk against the bright sky. In her mind it was associated with unbearable heartbreak, countless tears and an anguished letting go of loved ones. She had always felt a sadness in that place, and now it drew her to it. Her feet seemed to move of their own volition, carrying her unerringly across the grown-over path to the long-deserted building.

She hesitated, then slipped in the sagging opening left by a warped door. It was dank and dark, cobwebby and faintly musty. At first glance, it seemed empty, and yet she sensed it was not and waited for her eyes to adjust the blackness to grey.

She saw him, his outline emerging a darker shade against the dimensionless, ghostly grey. For the second time that night, she had an eerie sensation of living moments she had already lived. He sat on an overturned apple bin, his shoulders hunched, his head cradled in his hands.

"Reed."

His head snapped up. "Go away," he ordered, his voice faintly raspy.

She ignored the command, some instinct making her move closer to him. It was also pure instinct that made her reach out and touch his arm, lightly and gently. It was like a plaster casing had crumbled from around him—the stone god was replaced with a man of flesh and blood, heart and soul. His face, before he averted it from her, was tortured.

"Reed, what's wrong?" Her own heartache was muffled by the expression on his face, and she could not prevent herself from showing concern or ignore the fact that she *needed* to comfort him.

The silence was long, and when he spoke, his voice wrenched at her heart. It was not the voice of a calm, cool and collected man. His voice was a raspy whisper that broke here and there.

"It's even harder this time," he finally said, and then laughed, a humourless, hollow sound. "And it was the hardest thing I've ever done."

"What was?" she whispered.

He gave her a look of mingled anger and pain. "What do you think?" He looked away from her. "Sending you away."

She gasped. The hand that had been resting on his arm moved to her mouth, and she watched him wide-eyed. "That's not true," she stammered. "You know it's not true. You were hard and cold and mean—" But, painfully, something Mrs. K had said suddenly sprang into her mind—about Reed hiding his emotions behind a cool impenetrable mask of uncaring. His despair, his heartaches, his feelings were locked away in some untouchable place deep inside of him. Except, she could touch that place—

His gaze was locked on her face. "How could I have been anything else?" he demanded softly. "What would you have done if you knew the truth? If you had ever guessed how hard it was? If I had slipped for even an instant, and you had guessed it was love, would you have gone? No, you would have been all over me and then I could have never made you go—I could have never let you go."

The anger faded from his eyes, leaving only the pain. He looked away from her. "Do you know how much love it takes to do something like that? To send away someone who is as much a part of you as the air you breathe?"

She gazed at that strong, proud profile with tear-misted eyes. "If you loved me, how could you?" *And how can you?*

"Spring...oh, Spring." His voice was weary and patient. "How do you think it feels for a mature man to discover he's in love with an eighteen-year-old girl? In love, suddenly and without warning, to a young woman who sprang, just as suddenly and without warning, from a little girl?

"There you were, half child, half woman, offering everything to me, when you didn't even know what you were offering. Don't you understand it was love that made me refuse it? Can't you understand how much love it took to let you remain a child for a little while longer? To let you grow up slowly and to wait for you, instead of rushing you into a role you weren't ready for? To take what you offered me that night would have been an act of unforgivable selfishness—not an act of love.

"It would have robbed you of a part of growing up, and it would have robbed me of my self-respect. The fact that I was so tempted almost did that anyway. I'd look in the mirror and wonder where the hell the perverted side in my nature had come from.

"So I made you go, Spring. For you. For me. I made it hard and cruel because you had to go—and because I knew you'd be safe from me as long as you thought you hated me. Safe to grow up. Then when you graduated from college and didn't come home, I started to wonder if by loving you I had lost you forever. I wanted to be patient. I wanted you to taste all of life that you wanted, so that when you came home, you would never wonder if you'd missed something."

He stopped and looked at his hands, seeming surprised that they were clenching and unclenching in tense fists.

"Then I made the mistake I told you about this afternoon. You see, I told myself that I was only going to Vancouver to make sure you were all right and to make sure you were happy. I told myself that would be enough. But it wasn't. Maybe it would have been if you had looked happy, but you looked tired, sick and sad, and I nearly died for loving you. I'd nearly forgotten how bittersweet it was—how it made me feel joyous, mixed-up, jealous and angry all at once. But mostly, I just wanted to get you home where I could look after you. I promised myself I wouldn't push you or pressure you to love me—that I wouldn't do anything to influence you or try to resurrect the childhood crush you had on me. I didn't want you to love me in that way anymore—even if that's what I missed every single day you were gone.

"So I waited, Spring. I've waited for you to love me freely and of your own choosing. At first I thought I had a chance. And then I saw you wilting before my eyes. And it's not love to capture something, to insist on keeping it only to watch captivity drain it of its spirit, joy, beauty...."

He gave her a resigned, strained smile. "I wasn't going to tell you any of this," he confessed wearily. "It's an unfair burden to lay on you. You shouldn't have come in here. I could have managed to keep up the pretense that I didn't care so that you could have gone without guilt."

He's telling me he loves me, she thought with dazed wonder, and life leapt within her, opening like a joyous flower stretching toward the sun after a long and drenching rain.

"Don't you think there's been quite enough pretense?" she asked him gently. "Reed, I love you. I love you with all my heart and soul." She smiled, not wiping away the tears that danced down her cheeks. "And you're quite right—I'll never go now."

He was on his feet in an instant, looking down at her, his face once again chiselled in the stone of fierce pride. "I don't need your pity, Spring! You're leaving. Do you take me for an idiot? Don't you think I know what it means when a woman starts prancing around in fancy clothes, putting on makeup and fooling with her hair? It means she's bored and restless and looking for something. If I could have given you that something, I would have known by now—and I sure as hell won't let you hang around here because you feel guilty that I was dumb enough to fall for a woman ten years younger than me— or because of your misplaced sense of duty or debt. You don't owe me anything."

"You are an idiot," she informed him tenderly, and when his face tightened like she had poured salt into a raw wound, she could no longer resist putting her arms around him. He stiffened and then surrendered, his arms creeping around her.

"Why are you doing this to me?" he muttered hoarsely.

"Reed, I love you."

He looked down at her with frank and cynical disbelief, yet couldn't quite seem to bring himself to let her go.

"Do you know why I was prancing around in fancy clothes, as you put it? Because I was trying to get you to notice me. I was trying to be what I thought a woman should be to deserve a man like you. I thought I wasn't feminine enough or mature enough or—"

The cynicism faded from his face and was replaced with a look so magnificently tender and cherishing, she thought she would die for the sheer beauty of it.

"You were trying to change . . . for me?" he asked incredulously. "Spring, you were only eighteen years old when I recognized you were all the woman I could ever want. It's true that then it was like a tiny closed bud, but it's also true that I knew what its opening would be like. I saw men all around me settle for superficial things in relationships, and I knew that's not what I wanted. In you I saw a woman who could be more than a decoration for my arm, a conquest to show off to my friends, someone to cook my meals, clean my house. In you I saw a woman who could be my companion, my partner, my friend, my lover." He smiled. "I almost let that slip one day. Penny asked why I wasn't making a fuss about you working in the orchard. I caught myself and said it was because you grew up here—but what almost came out was that you belonged here, at my side, as my soul mate for all time."

His arms tightened around her, and his lips rained small kissed down on her hair. The barn must have suddenly seemed too dark and brooding because he swooped her up in strong arms and then set her down in a yard washed in moonlight.

"I wouldn't change one single thing about you. Not one." He paused, ran a wondering finger over the curve of her flushed cheek, then smiled. "Well, maybe one."

She knew how bad she was at changing, and she knew what she had decided about pretending, so she looked at him fearfully. "What?" she asked with trepidation.

"I want to change your marital status. Soon. Very soon."

She laughed, and the sound tinkled like a thousand tiny bells singing yes. Reed's gaze caught on her lips, and with a fierce groan, his head dropped over hers, and he took them for his own.

The porch light came on abruptly, pulling them out of a silver-washed world that had nothing to do with the moon.

"And if it isn't about time," Mrs. K said, standing on the porch, her hands on her hips. "I've never seen such a pair of self-sacrificing nincompoops in all my born days." She regarded them sternly, and shook a finger at them. "But I won't have any hanky-panky before the wedding."

"You're fired," Reed called over his shoulder with mock severity, his eyes never leaving Spring's face. An astoundingly girlish giggle floated across the lawn, and the light snapped out. Reed's lips came home to Spring's once more . . . and the dream began.

COMING NEXT MONTH

LOGAN'S WOMAN—Glenda Sands
Susan belonged to another man—or so Clark Haggerty thought. And
it was up to Susan to reinforce that belief. But that was easier said
than done once she found herself falling in love with him.

TOMORROW'S DAWN—Frances Lloyd
Justine Carroll had once loved Marcus Glendinning, but he had
married another woman. Now he had returned, determined to win her
back. Did he deserve another chance?

LADY AND THE LEGEND—Sharon De Vita
Victoria Fairchild was a lady—even though she wasn't acting like one.
It couldn't have anything to do with Gator McCallister—could it?

BENEATH A SUMMER MOON—Juli Greene
Raising two sons and running a garden center kept widow
Janice Haley busy, but she longed for a man to make her feel like a woman
again. Why did that man have to be the impossible David Phillips?

KISSING GAMES—Pamela Toth
Supernerd or Superman? When Patricia MacGregor first saw
Brad McKinney, she almost died. This was her dream date? Oh, no!
Then Brad set out to remind her that Clark Kent was only a
disguise—what was underneath was the real thing.

STRANGE ENCHANTMENT—Annette Broadrick
One enchanted evening, teacher Elizabeth Bannister saw ad executive
Dan Morgan across a crowded room. Mesmerized, both of them
knew that their lives would never be the same again.

AVAILABLE THIS MONTH:

SATIN AND WHITE LACE
Barbara Turner

DARE TO DREAM
Cara Colter

THE PROPER MISS PORTER
Ruth Langan

PURSUED BY LOVE
Caty Lear

SUGAR AND SPICE
Debbie Macomber

THE PRIVATE GARDEN
Arlene James

Breathtaking adventure and romance
in the mystical land of the pharaohs...

YESTERDAY AND TOMORROW

ERIN YORKE

A young British archeologist, Cassandra Baratowa, embarks
on an adventurous romp through Egypt in search of Queen
Nefertiti's tomb—and discovers the love of her life!

Available in MARCH, or reserve your copy for February shipping by sending your
name, address, zip or postal code along with a check or money order for $4.70 (in-
cludes 75¢ for postage and handling) payable to Worldwide Library to:

In the U.S.	In Canada
Worldwide Library	Worldwide Library
901 Fuhrmann Blvd.	P.O. Box 609
Box 1325	Fort Erie, Ontario
Buffalo, NY 14269-1325	L2A 9Z9

Please specify book title with your order.

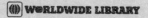 **WORLDWIDE LIBRARY**   YES-1

FOUR UNIQUE SERIES FOR EVERY WOMAN YOU ARE...

Silhouette Romance

Heartwarming romances that will make you laugh and cry as they bring you all the wonder and magic of falling in love.

6 titles per month

Silhouette Special Edition

Expanded romances written with emotion and heightened romantic tension to ensure powerful stories. A rare blend of passion and dramatic realism.

6 titles per month

Silhouette Desire

Believable, sensuous, compelling—and above all, romantic—these stories deliver the promise of love, the guarantee of satisfaction.

6 titles per month

Silhouette Intimate Moments

Love stories that entice; longer, more sensuous romances filled with adventure, suspense, glamour and melodrama.

4 titles per month

Silhouette Romances
not available in retail outlets in Canada

SIL-GEN-1A